The Other Side of the Circle

Dr. J. Oliver Johnson

ISBN: 0692340637
ISBN-13: 978-0692340639

Negative
Imprint

"The boundaries which divide Life from Death are at best shadowy and vague. Who shall say where the one ends, and where the other begins?"

Edgar Allan Poe

INTRODUCTION:
A CONVERSATION OF THE ARTS

"Your mother's a whore who sells her body to crippled alcoholics."

These words would bring rage to the eyes of any young school boy when taunted on the playground by the class bully, but they don't hurt so bad when they come from your own father, just as they have to me for the past twenty-three years. And it shows at least a little bit of credibility when he sits before me a crippled alcoholic.

Before today, I hadn't seen my mother since before I could remember, but from the stories my father has told me my whole life, I feel as though

I've known her all along.

"She ain't nothing but a cheatin' whore and all she ever wants from anybody is their money." He was always so straight-forward and unapologetic when he spoke of my roots, both maternal and paternal. "She couldn't even get a decent guy to pay for her. Had to go after the drunk ones that ain't got no legs."

He reached down and repositioned himself in his wheelchair in a way that would better enable him to reach his whiskey, which he drank from a glass now so he could mix it with a little bit of water. He's been trying to cut back on the liquor lately, and it's hard to do that while drinking straight out of the bottle.

I'm always proud when he tries to go sober, but I think this round of the battle will be lost quicker than most of the previous bouts. Self-pity is a powerful beast that takes many forms, and it always has a ferocious thirst. For now, the beast is in a shallow sleep, but I believe it's just about time for it to awaken.

"I know, I know," I responded in a low tone, almost under my breath. "I'm real proud of her, too."

"I'm sure you are," he snapped back. "You got about the same taste in girls that she had in men. Only she didn't care about legs, and you go after the darkest ones you could find. Hope you never knock that one up. Have yourself a little gray baby. Probably name him after me, too. Just to twist that knife around a little more in my back."

My father took every decision I ever made as a direct insult, even when it never had anything to do with him. He was almost glad to hear that I started dating a girl I had met at college, but the disapproval came down like acid rain when he found out she was black. He was never a racist before — hell, some of his old drinking buddies were black — but he became David Duke around me after that devastating revelation.

"What the hell did she want, anyway?" He was finally speaking again after concentrating hard on the bottle, the glass, and those damned little ice cubes.

"Oh, you know. Just some fried chicken and watermelon," I shot back with unmistakable sarcasm.

"No, not your damned Mandingo wench. Your hooker mother," he slurred his scream. "What the hell did she want? Come knockin' on my front door when I wasn't even home. And she's lucky I wasn't home. Would've kicked her right in the ass."

He grinned a little as he rubbed his legs at their ends, just above where his knees should be. Then he finished off the glass and began to mix himself another drink.

"She was looking for me," I explained to him as he missed his glass and dropped two ice cubes onto the floor. He'll just grind them into the carpet later with his wheelchair. "She looked up the name in the phone book and thought it was my address."

"She probably didn't think I'd be living in a second-floor apartment. Didn't figure I'd make it up here on my own." He amused himself with her casual and blatant underestimation of his abilities.

"She probably didn't see the elevator at the end of the building." I wasn't trying to knock him off of his cloud completely, but I did my best to roll him a little closer to the edge. "Besides, she probably figured you'd be dead by now. Either drank yourself to death or flung yourself back into oncoming traffic. Don't worry; I gave her my correct address, so I doubt you'll see her around this heap again."

The old man slammed his empty glass down onto the end table he often used as his personal bar while he watched television or read a book. He had plenty of money coming in from government and insurance checks so he hasn't had to work a day since his accident. Not that he'd be able to hold down a job, anyway. There's not much he could do from a wheelchair except be an office worker, and that just isn't something he could force himself to become.

"You know she gave you up so she could continue doing drugs and whoring herself out to truck drivers?" he continued the one-sided argument. "You know she didn't even spell your name right?"

He made it sound like a question, but he was just trying to cut her credibility even shorter, as if he knew she was only here to pull some sort of scam on either me or him.

"Yeah, but you could have legally changed the spelling of it, maybe even given me a middle name, but you decided to just nickname me after a folk singer. And he's not even a singer; he's a folk mumbler!"

"Dylan is a fine name," he fought back. "Besides, I didn't have the $850 to pay to have your name changed, Junior."

He never referred to me as "Junior" except in sarcasm when talking about my mother's decision to name me after the only paying customer to ever get her pregnant.

"No, you had the money, but you just drank it away. Other fathers save money to help put their kids through a decent college ..."

"Other fathers have legs!" he shouted so loudly his voice almost cracked. "When you was little, you wanted to join the Air Force. They would've put you through college."

He tried to turn everything around and make me feel completely responsible for my past, so the fact that my life isn't already mapped out for me on a street of gold is entirely my fault.

"Well, we're going out to dinner tonight and we'd both like for you to come with us. We all have a lot to talk about." I spoke calmly as I tried to change the subject. Those same old conversations always end with one of us leaving angry. This time I would be leaving, but he would be the angry one.

"I knew that woman for one night and it already cost me more than all that money I gave her," he spoke in a remorseful, almost vibrating tone, losing himself in thoughts of regret for his one biggest mistake in life. "No, you go on ahead. I already made plans."

I stood up and walked to the door. I turned the knob before stopping and turning back to him, almost bringing myself to ask him to change his mind. He saw my hesitation to leave and immediately picked up the bottle and chugged the whiskey straight from the top.

I kept on, closing the door behind me without another word to him.

PART ONE

DR. J. OLIVER JOHNSON

CHAPTER ONE:
A FATHER'S RECOLLECTION

I say the biggest turning point in my life was when I got drunk enough and lonely enough to pay that hooker for a ride in her hotel room. Anybody else would take one look at me, notice my most prominent physical feature, and say otherwise. But that night with that hooker changed everything for the worse, even more so than my life's previous major turning point. I wish I never saw that damn hooker. That's where all of my problems began.

But everything that happens to someone is a result of something else that has already happened, which put them in a position for the shit to just keep piling up on them. For example, if I never would've been drunk that night, I never would've gotten with that hooker. And if there was something other than the Spurs game on the television that night, I never would've went to the liquor store so I could get drunk. And if I still had my legs, I would've been playing basketball myself or flying jet planes for the Air Force, so I wouldn't have needed to get drunk.

Either way, one bad move led to another until I was laying on my back, being ridden by some dirty hooker in the hotel room she lived in. After we were finished, she just rolled over, lit up a cigarette and passed out cold. When I realized she was asleep, I took the cigarette out of her hand, climbed back into my chair and wheeled myself home.

If I had known then the kind of hell she would put me through in the years to come, I would've let that cigarette find its way into the cheap bed coverings. I would have gone home just the same, but that evil hooker would have been burnt up like the witch she is.

When I was a boy, my old man retired from the Air Force as a full-bird colonel. He flew for his whole career until he started teaching pilots. Flying was all he ever talked about, and so that is all I ever wanted to do.

I was tall and strong and smart. I lead the high school basketball team to a district championship and was on my way to a basketball scholarship, which I would've passed up. The Air Force was going to put me through college and then teach me to fly planes.

I had friends and a car and a girl, and I planned to marry her before joining the military. Her dad was also on his way to retiring from the Air Force, so she was used to the life and she wanted to join me during my quest to become a modern military hero.

We were considered part of the social elite at school, though barely anybody voted for us in the election for our prom king and queen. We didn't care, and most of the school hated us because we treated them like shit. We didn't give a fuck who the king or queen was; we just wanted to enjoy life like most kids do. But with prom right around the corner, something happened to me that took everything I had away.

I was eighteen years old and I knew that my freedom was almost within reach. Sure, I'd start off as the low man on the Air Force totem pole, but I would soon have everything I ever wanted. Not that I didn't already have everything I wanted up to that point.

My parents spoiled me with all that a young man needed to enjoy life, and they either didn't care or were too blind to see that I spent more time drinking, smoking and going to parties than I did studying or really doing anything else. Producing good grades came easily for me, especially since no teacher was going to let me get kicked off the basketball team for having less-than-perfect grades. At that age, I had the perfect life, and I thanked God every day that He was watching over me. At the time, I thought God would really take care of me forever.

I guess maybe my dad was just driving too fast for God to keep up that day, or maybe it was just God's day off. Either way, a quiet Sunday morning turned into a life of hell when me and a friend of mine went with my dad and a couple of his buddies on a fishing trip. The old men rode in my dad's truck while I drove my new Mustang behind them.

The day up to that point had been relatively uneventful. Church was as boring as it ever was and the weather couldn't have been more bland. We fished, drank some beer, and then decided to head home. Dad's truck made it out of the brush just fine, but the Mustang didn't have the ground clearance. Looking back, I don't know how I ever got the car in there in the first place.

Neither one of us had a chain or a rope in our vehicle, so we made the plan to all ride back in his truck, and me and my father would return later that evening with the proper tools to dig my car out.

"Climb in the back, Arthur," he chuckled for his friends. He made me and my friend, Chris, ride in the back like dogs while him and his pals laughed it up inside the cab.

Once we hit the freeway, my dad started swerving the truck, which made for an uncomfortable ride for me and Chris but a source of amusement for my dad and his buddies. The ice chest with the fish started sliding around the front of the bed, spilling some of the putrid water out. I moved toward the rear of the truck and leaned my back against the tailgate, hoping the smell of the fish wouldn't transfer onto my new clothes, which were still relatively clean by then.

Without any sort of warning at all, the tailgate flung itself open and I tumbled out of the truck and onto the freeway below. I remember the white light that flashed inside my head as my skull crashed against the road.

When I awoke, it was two days later. I had tubes and wires coming out all over my body and going into about a dozen different machines. I still had a headache, but I no longer had my legs. They were shredded apart by the force of an 18-wheeler that came skidding to a grinding halt right on top of me. I didn't even have my knees anymore. All I had were these two stumps. And that's the first thing anybody ever notices about me anymore.

Needless to say, my relationship with God came to an abrupt end, as did any of my plans for a future. Having no legs means not playing any basketball, and it sure as fuck means never flying any airplanes for the Air Force.

I blamed my father for the accident. I had to

blame somebody; I couldn't accept the fact that some things just happen that nobody could ever expect or prevent. And it didn't help that he just kept trying to convince me that my life wasn't over.

My mother just wanted me to make peace with my old man, saying that it wasn't his fault and that God has reasons for everything he chooses for us. I knew that this was all bullshit, and I basically pushed myself further away from them until I really had no parents left at all.

My girlfriend stopped coming around, too. She blamed it on my attitude problems and the hatred that grew inside of me since the accident. She said that she was more than willing to wait for me to recover mentally, but that she just didn't see that happening and my attitude toward her was hurtful. I tried to explain to her that my attitude was just a natural part of having my legs ripped from my body and that I never hated anybody who didn't deserve to be hated. Either way, she couldn't stand to see me anymore and took to instead seeing some other guy who asked her to the prom when he heard that I wouldn't be taking her. She declined his invitation because she didn't want to hurt my feelings, but they were an official couple just a week or so later. The last I heard about them is that he does construction in Austin and she stays at home, taking care of all their kids. Good for them, I say. They just did what they thought was right for them, and there's no sense in wishing them anything bad.

I kinda stopped talking to the rest of my friends, too. The only person I couldn't drive away from me permanently was Father Silva from the church I attended right up until the day of the accident. That's not to say that I didn't try my best to keep him away, though. I called both him and God every swear word in the book. I even ripped a bible apart when he tried to force me to read something out of it that was supposed to make me understand why God chose for me to be a couple of feet shorter now.

"Don't look at me as a priest," he told me. "Look at me as you would any of your other friends."

"But I ain't got no other friends now," I'd shoot back. "Your God sent them away, too."

"No, I think that was mostly your choice," he'd explain calmly. "Besides, God has chosen me to stay and continue being your friend." Father Silva was such a conniving bastard, and I made sure to let him know it.

He convinced my parents to give me my space, and they helped me move my stuff out of their house and into my own apartment after my legs stopped bleeding through the bandages and I had convinced myself that I could function independently.

I had missed so much school that I couldn't simply pick up where I had left off, so I basically dropped out after the accident toward the end of my senior year and never got around to going back the next year. I had always planned on going back and graduating through some sort of adult program, but those plans just always seemed to fall through the cracks somewhere and are now lying right next to my basketball scholarship, my Air Force career and my pair of walking shoes.

With the money I had coming in from my insurance checks and my permanent disability benefits, I had plenty of income to live off of. There wasn't a whole lot left for entertainment purposes, but I couldn't do a whole hell of a lot, anyway. I found that drinking was cheap, as well as enjoyable, and until I turned the legal age to buy booze, the Arabs down at the corner market would sell to me because I'd always cash my welfare checks there. I even used food stamps there for a few years until they made the process of getting them tedious enough to force me to give up on them. I rarely used them to buy food, anyway. I'd buy booze and cigarettes. That wasn't legal, but those dirty sand monkeys knew of some loop-hole that allowed them to sell the food stamps back to the government for more than what they lost by allowing people like me to use them on whatever we wanted.

It's not like I had much food to buy, anyway. Father Silva put my name on the church's list of recipients of their meal delivery program. Through donations, the church was able to provide food for needy members of the church.

Even when I made sure my cabinets and refrigerator had plenty of food, Father Silva would still bring more by. He was the only one who would deliver it because I'd threaten to shoot anyone who came by to deliver me their pity. Father Silva was the only one to recognize that these were hollow threats. He said that I was one of God's children who lost my way. Everyone else at the church just said that I was a lost cause. Also, Father Silva knew that I didn't own a gun, nor had I ever shot one before.

Father Silva would invite himself over to my apartment and make dinner just about every Thanksgiving, Christmas and Easter, and he learned to do so without the praying and religious bullshit. But he did go so far as to steal my spare apartment key and let himself in when I wasn't home. I'd come back from the corner store or the bar only to find more food and the occasional book on spiritual guidance sitting there waiting for me. Out of complete boredom, I'd sometimes read the books, but I never let him know it. He eventually returned the key, but only after making a copy of it for himself. This went on for years until I finally started going back to the church.

I went out of desperation that first time I returned. I had drank up all my whiskey the night before and wheeled myself down to the corner store, only to find that it had closed down because those towel heads broke too many liquor laws and the Texas Alcoholic Beverage

Commission forced them to close up. I had to keep wheeling down to the supermarket, but they refused to sell me any booze before noon on Sundays because of some bullshit state law. Realizing it was too far for me to go home just to return again a few hours later, I decided to take a stroll around some streets that I hadn't ventured onto since I was a kid.

I rolled past the house I grew up in. Some Mexicans lived in it now. It was apparent by the little gnome statues in the unkempt lawn and the clothesline in the front yard with the gaudy shirts hanging from it that no decent white person would be caught dead wearing. My parents had sold the house a few years back and moved to Florida so they could enjoy their retirement. They asked me to go with them and they offered to help me find a place near them if I didn't want to move into their house. I politely declined their offer. Only San Antonio, a place that recognizes anybody from the overweight to the just plain lazy as handicapped, would allow me to live with the comfort that I had grown accustomed to in the years following the accident. If I moved anywhere else, I'd be forced to look for a job.

I wheeled myself through the church doors and interrupted Father Silva's sermon. He wasn't bothered by the squeaky door penetrating the otherwise calm air, but when he looked up and saw that it was me, he lost his place on the pad of paper he was using as notes. It was as if a ghost had just walked in, except this ghost glided in on rubber tires and remained seated.

I found a spot in the back where I could make a quick escape if he was going to try to introduce me to the congregation. I was sure very few of them still remembered who I was, anyway. But he never did. Instead, he just found his place and continued his sermon. When he was finished, I was the first one back out the door as I headed quickly back to the supermarket. If I hurried, I'd get there just at noon, and that skinny little bitch behind the register wouldn't be able to refuse my purchase.

When I got home, there was a note on my refrigerator from Father Silva, simply inviting me back next week. I crumpled it up and threw it away. Then I poured myself a drink and turned on the television. Every channel had some televangelist trying to tell me that I was a sinner, but I'd had enough of God for one day, so I popped a tape of *Pat Garret and Billy the Kid* into the VCR. The movie was horrible and not historically accurate at all, but Bob Dylan's attempt at acting always made me laugh, and that's just what I needed right then.

I always made sure to stock up on booze from then on so that I wouldn't have to wait until noon on Sundays to start my drinking. I just wasn't worth a damn until I had just a little bit of the juice flowing through my veins, and to sleep-in was just out of the question. No matter how drunk I was the night before, whenever the sun came up, so I did. No matter how thick of a blanket I hung over all the windows in my tiny, shit-hole apartment, I could still feel the sun peaking around and poking me in the face, saying, "Get up, you legless fuck. Beauty sleep ain't gonna do you no good, anyhow."

But the truth is I got curious about the church. I remember that I might have enjoyed it as a kid. I was young and naïve back then, but maybe if I'd go back now, I might actually forget my common sense and actually have something to enjoy again other than the booze. And maybe I'll stop having thoughts of wheeling myself back out onto the loop and letting the freeway speeders finish what they started all them years ago. Maybe my chair would shred their tires. Fuck 'em. Serves 'em all right for taking my legs in the first place. And as much as I missed my legs, thinking about the freeway made me miss my old Mustang even more.

When I left home, I left the car there with my parents. I couldn't use it anymore. But when they took off to Florida, they dropped it off in the parking lot of my apartment in perfect running order and with current registration stickers. My dad said something about how maybe I could take it in and have some of those special hand controls installed so I could drive again. Instead, I sold it for a pretty good chunk of change and put the money in the bank. A classic Mustang in excellent condition with low miles is a rare find. Anyone who gets a beauty like that drives it until the wheels fall off. "There ain't no way you can keep me from racing my 'Stang," any proud owner would say to his envious admirers.

Well, how about if they cut off both of your fucking legs? Then you'd roll your crippled ass around town in a damn chair, you little shit! And forget about the bitches. The ones who fling their pussies around like boomerangs to everyone else wouldn't even jerk you off in a dark parking lot anymore. No, you gotta pay for it like the rest of us cripples. And you'll have to pay big. Fucking a freak costs extra. Pretty soon, you'll stop even worrying about it. Screwing won't seem as important anymore. You'll even stop buying porn videos at the liquor store so you could buy even more booze. Sometimes you'll long for a woman who looks even half-decent to say hello, or even smile at you as they hurry around you on the sidewalk. It'll turn into years since you can remember the feel of a woman, the smell of her hair, her soft breath on your neck as you hold her against your body.

Fuck it. Go buy more booze.

After a few weeks, I decided to roll back to church. Father Silva had been by probably two or three times since that Sunday. He hadn't been coming by as often as he used to, and I was beginning to miss having someone around for me to talk shit to.

I didn't get there in time to catch his sermon, so I snuck in through the side door as everyone else was leaving out the front door, saying their weekly goodbyes to Father Silva. I don't know what I was expecting to do once I got there, so I decided to hurry into a confession booth and wait to be heard. After about fifteen minutes, I heard his footsteps as he walked almost completely past the booths. I coughed so that he knew someone was inside. I heard his footsteps come closer, pause, and then he opened his door and sat down inside.

I wasn't too familiar with the proper confession procedures, other than what I had seen in the movies. Before he could speak, I started.

"Forgive me, Father, for I have sinned," I said in a low, disguised voice. "It's been a while since I've been here."

"Go on," he replied. His tone reminded me of how the nurses tried to coax me down the halls of the hospital for the first time in that damn wheelchair. "I'm listening."

"Well, I took the Lord's name in vain" That was all I could think of to say.

"I see. Can you tell me what brought this on? Was it anger? Were you angry at someone, maybe yourself, or maybe at God?"

"Oh, Father, I'm just so worried that I'll never be able to walk next to Jesus in Heaven." I was really laying it on thick, and it was actually the most fun I'd had in quite a while, I'm sad to say.

"The Lord doesn't appreciate you taking His name in vain, I assure you, but I really don't think it would keep you out of Heaven. But that's only if you're sorry for doing it, and I think that you are. That is why you are here right now."

"No, no, Father. You don't understand. I'll never get to walk beside Jesus." I put a little whine into it for effect.

"And why do you think this?"

"Because I ain't got no goddamn legs!" I began to howl with a laughter that surprised even myself, and it filled the pews with the sound of a man possessed.

I heard the door open on his side of the booth and I thought he had left in disgust. As his door came to a slam, I was coming out of my laughter.

"You fuckin' cripple," he scolded. I was stunned silent. I thought he had left. What was he doing when he had opened the door, checking for witnesses? "What the hell are you doing here?"

I had never heard Father Silva even raise his voice before, let alone cuss. As strong-willed and defiant as I have always thought myself as being, his response shut me up fast.

"Just because you've turned your back on God doesn't mean that He has turned His back on you!" Now he just sounded evil. "Get the hell out of here before I push your damned chair down the front steps."

"But, Father Silva," I started, eager to sincerely

apologize.

"I said to get the fuck out!" He seemed just short of taking the Lord's name in vain himself, massaging back an impending migraine with his palm through that damned scar above his eye while he obviously contemplated launching my chair down the steps. So I just wheeled myself outside and down the handicap ramp and started my trip back home.

Once there, I put on a tape of Bob Dylan's *John Wesley Harding* album and drank myself into lunch time. And for lunch, I had more to drink.

Out of all the bad things I'd done in my life, out of all the people I hurt and drove away, the only one I really felt bad about was Father Silva. After my friends stopped coming around, after my parents moved to Florida and stopped writing, it was Father Silva who stuck around. And it was always Father Silva who I abused the most with my anger and resentment. It wasn't him that I was even mad at. It was God. And now even Father Silva hated me.

I don't recall exactly how long it took me to drink up everything in my apartment, but I know it wasn't very long at all. I had no more booze in my cupboards, but if I left home I knew I'd just find a way back onto the freeway. I wouldn't need a note. Nobody would read it, anyway. And anyone who knew me would know exactly what I was doing on the loop when the next semi truck plowed into me.

I turned on the television, but all that was on was a Spurs basketball game. The Lakers were kicking the shit out of the Spurs and I knew there was no chance for a comeback. If I had been able to take that basketball scholarship, maybe the Spurs would've drafted me. I'd be their only hope against the Lakers. And I'd be rich. And I'd have women. And I'd be walking tall.

I turned off the tube and put a shirt on. I was off to the freeway, but first I'd stop at the liquor store. The Arabs got their store back open, and I knew they'd be happy to see their best customer again.

I rolled through the narrow aisles and selected my usual brand of whiskey, and as I rolled up to the counter, I was met by the ass and legs of an angel. Being confined to the chair gave me one advantage, which was that it put my eyes at the same height as her ass — her ass, which belonged to an angel.

She wasn't really an angel. As it turned out, she was a filthy fuckin' prostitute. Even through the initial infatuation, I could tell that she was a working girl by the leather mini-skirt and the high-heeled shoes. Her tight halter top with the leopard print accentuated her large breasts, and her bright red lipstick accentuated her luscious lips. I had always dreamed of being with a woman as beautiful as her, but when I dreamed, I never had to pay for it. And I always had my legs. As she paid for her cigarettes and walked outside, I could feel my pants tighten at the fly.

"She new here," one of the Arabs said to me in his half-English, half-camel language. "She here when store open back up. I tell her no one here pays for hook, but she stay on corner all over the night. No man pay her for do it yet. Not for three day she is here."

I paid for my bottle and my smokes and I hurried to the door. With any luck I'd get another look at her before she was gone, walking down the street to some other corner where it might be easier for her to find a customer. In that case, I'd follow her from a distance, just close enough to watch her rear end trying its best to work its way out of that tiny skirt. Maybe I'd be there to catch it when it falls out. But probably not. She probably didn't even notice me inside the store, and if she catches me following her, she'd probably mace me and steal my wallet and whiskey.

As I passed through the exit, she was gone. She wasn't to the left, and not to the right. And she wasn't across the street, neither. Maybe it was for the best, I thought. After all, a hooker with poor business skills like her might just as well stab me before I had a chance to turn down her business proposal.

I was on my way to the loop, anyway, but first a cigarette to dry the mouth a little. I never needed any help getting drunk, but I wanted to make sure to finish the entire bottle of booze as quickly as possible. I'd rather not see death's headlights, and I didn't want to change my mind once I got there again.

As I touched the flame of my lighter to the tip of my cigarette, I cocked my head to the left ever so slightly to avoid any wind that may be blowing through. Out of the corner of my eye I saw something slowly start to move closer.

"Can I borrow your lighter?" Her voice penetrated the air and the rest of the world went silent. She had been standing up against the wall, just outside the door. I must've rolled right past without seeing her. "My lighter's out of fluid and I didn't get any matches inside."

Normally, when anybody else had the nerve to ask me for a light, I'd tell them to go fuck themself. With her, however, I just held out my lighter for her to take. She slid her cigarette back between her scarlet lips and leaned into my hand. I struck up the flame, and watched as the cherry of her cigarette glowed a beautiful red and sizzled while she took in that initial drag.

She made smoking look sexy. She should give up screwing for money, I thought. Put her picture on a billboard across the street from a high school parking lot with her leopard print halter top and a freshly-lit cigarette. That would be good advertising, pure and simple. The tobacco companies would have a thousand new addicts by the end of the lunch period.

"You come here often?" she asked, trying to

be sexy, as if she needed to try at all. I didn't know what to say back to her, so I didn't say anything. "I'm new here. Not to this corner. I mean I'm new to San Antonio. I'm from El Paso. Do you come here often?"

"Yes," I squeezed out the solitary word. "Yes, I do. I mean I used to before they closed down the store. This is my first time back since it reopened."

"Yeah, I think I would've remembered you," she said through a sincere smile, not offending at all. "I've been here every night since it opened, I guess. It sure feels like a lot longer than only three nights, though. Do you live around here someplace?"

"No, it's a little bit away from here."

"Little bit of a walk, huh?" She looked back down at me and exhaled a deep breath, probably realizing the stupid comment. "Look, I'm staying in a hotel just around the corner from here. I'm just staying there for right now, renting by the week. Anyway, it's getting pretty cold out here, and it's supposed to get pretty low tonight. Do you wanna go back to my room so I can help you out with that bottle? I have ice cubes and paper cups. They came with the room."

I didn't know what to say. Usually, girls never even look at me, and this one was wanting to take me home. I knew that she was just trying to earn a living and that I was just another customer to her, but she made it all sound so good, like she really wanted me. When she looked down to me, she was never looking down *at* me. I never gave her any answer. She just smiled, turned around and started walking slowly down the sidewalk, like a model going back in from the end of the runway. I gave her a three-step lead, and then I caught up. I figured I'd have one last fling before I died, and then I'd be on my way to the freeway. Neither of us said another word the two blocks to her hotel room. When she closed the door behind us, however, she wasn't quite as shy anymore.

As I sat quietly, she told me all about her childhood, her life in El Paso, her recent move to San Antonio, and her hopes of starting over fresh, maybe as a waitress. She never specifically came right out and told me that she was a hooker, which actually made me feel safe. An undercover police officer would probably identify herself as a hooker first, just so there'd be no question about my intentions if I was to inquire about her services. So at least she wasn't a cop, I reasoned.

She never asked about my legs, so I never volunteered to tell her. I just kept drinking out of my paper cup and smoking my cigarettes. Toward the end of the bottle, we were both pretty buzzed and the room was filled with a heavy smoke. I noticed that she had taken apart the smoke detector and unplugged the alarm clock. After about two hours, she was sitting on my lap, and her tongue was finding its way to the back of my mouth.

I don't remember how I got onto the bed or how my clothes got onto the floor next to hers, but I do remember the way she straddled me like I was a raging bull, only it was her doing all the bucking. And because of all the alcohol in my blood stream, I was able to last more than eight seconds, though it probably wasn't a whole lot longer than that. It had been forever since I had even been close enough to smell a woman, and now we were sweating all over each other.

"More, more," she screamed.

It didn't last very long, but it was the best ride of my life. And after it was all over, she dismounted and lit up a cigarette. Then she laid down next to me, kissed my chest and she fell asleep on my arm. I laid there awake, staring at her while my right arm lost its blood circulation. I slid my arm out from under her, careful not to wake her up, and I continued to watch her sleep. I took the cigarette from her hand, took a drag and snuffed it out in the ash tray.

On the nightstand under the ashtray was some part of a song or something recently etched into the wood. I didn't recognize the lyrics, but I read them over and over in my head, trying hard to remember the song they belonged to or somehow understand the meaning of the words. It said something about obstacles in life, which is what caught my attention. Was this woman another obstacle, or was she a good thing?

Even with what she had just done to me, she

still looked like an angel. I began to wonder if she really liked me or if she was just a good actress. She was definitely a prostitute, but she had never mentioned anything about me paying her, and she didn't seem to mind that I stayed the night.

I began to see visions in my head of the both of us. I saw me at the dining room table, reading the newspaper. She was in the kitchen, wearing an apron and baking something in the oven.

I wondered if she would gather up her clothes and come back with me to my apartment if I asked her to. She said she was looking for a fresh start, and that would be a fresh start for the both of us. Soon, I was also asleep.

I don't know what time it was when I woke up because the alarm clock was still unplugged from the wall. Not knowing what else to do, I got myself dressed and sat in my chair, just wondering what I would even say to her if she woke up. I thought about how I would ask her to come home with me. She and I would go through life together and we'd both want nothing more than to be happy with our lives and we would each make sure that it happened for the both of us.

And then it all began to seem like a very bad idea. She would just laugh at me and call me a freak. She would demand to be paid for her night's work and probably mace me just for good measure. That's what would happen when she woke up sober, I just knew it.

I took all the cash from my wallet, probably around $200, and placed it on the nightstand next to the bed. Then I quietly rolled myself out the door and went home.

CHAPTER TWO:
A MOTHER'S INTUITION

My daddy used to fuck me when I was a little girl. And then my brothers started in on it when I got a little bit older. My mama wasn't around to make 'em stop. She hung herself from a leaky pipe in the roof of the basement when I was just little.

Her suicide note wasn't nothing but some bullshit poem about taking control of things and running into walls. It didn't make no sense, but at least I understood why she kicked out the stool.

I'm not saying that all of this is to blame for every bad decision that I've made in my life, but it didn't help me out none, neither. At the very least, it made it really difficult for me to know what a real family is supposed to look like.

All I can remember of my mother before she died is when she got the shit kicked out of her by my daddy. He liked to drink and he didn't care to work much. It always seemed like he was getting fired from every job he got just a few days after getting it. He never had any pride in himself or in his family, so he applied for every type of welfare there was to sign up for. And that is how we barely had enough to get by.

After my mother killed herself, he took to me real fast for his sex needs. I was just real little, but that didn't matter to him. Sometimes my brothers would watch if my daddy was to make it with me on the floor in the living room. And when they got old enough to know what to do, they'd come into my room at night, either one at a time or both at once, and they'd do me just like our daddy taught 'em. When I was eighteen, I left home and moved in with my boyfriend, Anthony.

I met Anthony at the truck stop that I was a waitress at. He was four years older than me, but I think I might have been a whole lot more mature than him. He'd been arrested once for some kind of robbery, but he only spent a few nights in jail before they let him out with probation. Other than that, he didn't ever cause no trouble with the law. But my daddy didn't like him on account that Anthony was a Mexican and I took to spending the night at his house every once in a while. Anyway, it didn't matter what my daddy thought of Anthony, because I stuffed all my clothes into a bag when I was eighteen and took 'em over to Anthony's house.

One day Anthony came home and told me to pack up my clothes again because we were going to San Antonio in a hurry. It was about an eight-hour drive from El Paso and he never did tell me why we were going there. I suspected at the time it was because he couldn't hold a decent job for very long and San Antonio had more opportunities for us. When we got into town, we went and checked into some old apartment building that used to be a hotel. The next day, we both got new jobs. Anthony was a mechanic of some kind and I was a waitress at a truck stop not too far from our apartment.

Everything was fine for a really long time. It was probably about a year that went by before it got bad again. We always paid our rent on time and we never went hungry and we even went to see a movie in the theater a couple of times. But one time, it must've been right about a year later, Anthony put all his clothes into the trunk of our car and said that he was going back to El Paso and that I wasn't going with him. He said that I was just keeping him down and that we weren't no good together. I cried for three days straight. And then the apartment manager came knocking because we were late with the rent money.

I was pretty popular at the truck stop. I'd

wiggle my ass and flirt with the guys and they'd give me a better tip. Some would joke with me and say it would be a good idea for me to go back with them to their trucks. So one time I agreed.

"Alright, Doyle," I answered back with a wry smile. "But that'll cost you more than just a three-dollar tip."

"Get your coat and meet me at my truck," he replied in a way that sounded like he had done this before with some other cute waitress. "It's the red Peterbilt parked next to the truck wash. I'm gonna hit the ATM first, and then I'm gonna see you out there."

I don't know if I was more proud of myself for taking a step toward getting the rent money or more disgusted with myself for selling my body to a greasy truck driver. I came to the quick conclusion that it didn't matter, anyhow. It was always taken from me, so why not make a quick buck off of it?

"And leave that apron on, sugar," Doyle said as he passed by me, his calloused right hand squeezing my ass as I fastened the buttons on my coat. "You know I love you in that apron."

I did things to him that most men couldn't even imagine, and the next morning I paid the rent.

It wasn't long before just about every lonely pusher coming through knew where to go for a cheap thrill. And it wasn't but a year or so before the attention got to be too much and my prick manager fired my ass. My hooking brought me in a whole lot more money, anyhow. My waitressing paycheck maybe paid for my food, and the tips were only good if I smiled when they pinched my ass or if I leaned forward far enough for them to peak down my shirt as I poured their coffee.

So, once again, I was at risk of being homeless unless I turned a trick here or there. After doing that for another year, I was still making just enough to be late with the rent every month. The longer I did it, the better I got at the business side of it all. I began to allow myself to just block out all emotion and simply do whatever the customer was willing to pay me to do, and I'd let him do to me whatever he wanted. And eventually, by lowering my price and increasing the tricks I'd pull each day, I was beginning to make a good amount of money. My rent stopped being late and I was saving to buy my own car. Then I planned to buy a bunch of nice clothes, get some books that teach you how to do professional jobs, and I was gonna try to get a job as a secretary or something like that. I'd be able to move into a real apartment and finally get my life going in a direction that I could be proud of.

But all of that was still some time away, and I just needed to keep on keeping on until I was able to leave this lifestyle behind for something better. All I needed was just a little bit more time.

And just like before, one single guy had to fuck it all up for me.

How could I have been so goddamn stupid? He was much too good looking to be dirty enough for a girl like me. His suit should have been a dead give-away that I wasn't really someone he wanted to bed down. He reeked of professionalism, more so than any man I had ever been with, and I'd been with some real professionals. If he was looking for high class, he would have done better to call up one of those escort services. Those girls had money, and so they made money. I was just trying to pay the rent.

"How much would it cost me to have sex with you?"

Ah, I get it now, I thought. He was new to this scene. No real degenerate would ask it like that. They all use sleazy innuendos, thinking it would be safer not to come right out and ask it, just in case I was an undercover police girl.

"How much is it worth to you?" I asked back. I didn't even hear what his answer was, but by the look of his suit, I knew it would be enough. And besides, I already did better business that night than I usually did, so I figured I'd just take whatever he offered without haggling over it like I usually did. I was gonna pop his cherry, so to speak. I'd give him a night to remember the rest of his life.

"Sounds good to me," I said through a smile after he named the price. "Gimme a ride to my apartment. It's just around the corner."

"Alright," he said, bashful as a puppy dog. "Hop in."

He didn't say a word the whole way back to my place, and all I could offer as conversation was directions to the front of my room. When he stopped the car, however, the peace was shattered by the blaring sirens and the flashing red and blue lights.

As they cuffed me, they read me my rights. Then they stuffed me in the back of the squad car. I had seen my father and brothers get arrested so many times, I just always thought it would be like déjà vu if it ever happened to me. But to tell the truth, I almost pissed my pants out of fear and embarrassment. I was so close to leaving that life behind to be a secretary or a receptionist, and now it was all over. After five years of working so hard at my goals, I wasn't gonna be a hooker *or* a secretary. I was on my way to becoming some Mexican lesbian's prison play toy, and there was nothing I could do about it.

I was still so naive that I just kept telling the cops over and over again that I hadn't done anything wrong, that the nice man was just giving me a ride home. Then I saw that nice man smiling and carrying on with the cops, not at all the shy, innocent boy who picked me up just fifteen minutes ago. How could I have been so fucking stupid!

Forty-five days later, I was back out on the street. My apartment was occupied by someone else since my rent had lapsed. I just knew that the apartment manager went through my stuff and took my money stash. I could tell the cops, but what would they have done about it? Even if I could prove that he had taken my money, I earned it all by hooking, and the cops would probably just spit on me and go about their business harassing poor people. I was back to square one, and I had very few options at that point. So I did one more night of hooking, and as soon as the bus station opened in the morning, I bought a one-way ticket back to El Paso.

I couldn't go back to my daddy's house, so I decided to try to find Anthony. Every time the bus stopped between San Antonio and El Paso, I made another phone call.

First I called Anthony's mom's old number. She gave me a number to where she thought Anthony was living now, but he didn't live there anymore. The man there gave me the number to the apartment manager, and I called him next. The manager gave me a forwarding number for Anthony, which was actually a number for Nick, who was mine and Anthony's friend a long time ago. Nick gave me a number to call, but said that he hadn't seen or talked to Anthony for a long time, so he didn't know if the number was still good or not. It turned out that it wasn't good anymore, so I called Nick back to see if he knew where else I could call to find Anthony. Nick said that he didn't know anywhere for me to look, but offered to pick me up at the bus station when I came in. He said that I could stay with him until I could find Anthony.

I never did find Anthony, and me and Nick eventually became a couple. I moved into his bedroom from the living room couch, and one day Nick asked me to marry him. He gave me a ring with a diamond on it that was bigger and shinier than anything I'd ever seen before. Nick made good money as a currier. He had a car and he bought another one for me. It was old and used, but I never had my own car before, so it was the better than any car I ever thought I'd ever have. Nick even asked all them other guys who were living in his house to move out so we could be alone as we try to start a family. And then one day, I found myself pregnant. Nick was happy, and I was finally getting my family started. We made plans to be married by a judge on Valentine's Day. The world was perfect for me and Nick in El Paso.

And then the cops ruined it again.

It was still early when they came knocking on the front door. I was sitting on the floor in front of the couch in my long shirt and socks, just watching my cartoons, when I heard them pounding. I don't usually answer the door, but I got up and opened it. There were about half a dozen cops standing around our porch, and some of them had their guns out. Then I heard a crash and the back door came flying around, and another half a dozen cops came running in with their guns out. They went running down the hall to drag out Nick as the first bunch of cops told me that they had a warrant to search the house and arrest Nick for transporting cocaine and selling it. I was shocked and scared, so I didn't say anything to them. After they brought Nick past me and out to the squad car, they told me to get dressed because I had to go answer some questions at the police station. They had a lady cop watch me as I got my pants on and then I went with them to another squad car and they drove me to the station.

They grilled me harder because of Nick than they did when it was me who was arrested for prostituting myself to an undercover cop. They said they found cocaine in our house and that they could arrest me and send me to prison for it. I told them that I was pregnant and that I don't use any drugs. They told me that they didn't give a fuck about me or my baby, and that if I went to prison, the baby would go to a foster home. Then they said that they would keep me out of jail if I signed a statement about how Nick was just holding the drugs for someone else. I knew the cocaine wasn't mine, and I also knew that Nick wouldn't want our baby born in prison, so I signed the statement. It was long and the cops said that they didn't have time for me to try to read and understand the whole thing. They said that the longer it took for me to sign it, the longer it would take to get Nick out on bond. I signed it, but they never let Nick out.

Nick went on and got convicted of selling and transporting the cocaine, and he was sentenced to ten years in prison. I tried to visit him in jail and in prison, but he refused to talk to me. The cops impounded both of the cars and I had to pawn my engagement ring to help pay the rent. My perfect life had been unraveled in just a few days and all I could think to do was go down to the corner bar.

I probably shouldn't have been drinking or smoking because of the baby, but it turns out that it didn't matter, anyway. The baby died in my belly because of the stress. That's what I figure, at least. So the cigarettes and bourbon didn't matter to it at all. I had to have it removed like an already dead abortion.

I didn't want the baby anymore, anyway. I couldn't raise it by myself, so I just thought that it was God's way of telling me to wait on starting up my family.

So now I had no baby and no man. I was back to square one again. I took everything from Nick's house and had a yard sale. Then I bought me a one-way ticket back to San Antonio.

I don't know what I was planning to do once I got back to San Antonio. I thought that maybe I could remember enough from grade school to go be a tour guide at the Alamo. No, probably not. I should've gotten a ticket in the other direction.

I've never tried New Mexico. The deserts in Arizona might actually be refreshing. Or maybe I could've been a movie star in California. It didn't matter, anyway. I had already sunk all my money into a ticket to San Antonio, and at least I knew what the people were like there. At least I knew they were real, not like all them faggot liberals in California. I was always good at making friends, so I could get along with the people anywhere, but at least I knew they were real in San Antonio.

Whatever my goals were, I knew that I had to go back to hooking for a little while, just long enough to get a place to stay and a bite to eat. Then I would quit again. I wouldn't need to do it for five more years this time. That's too long and it wasn't worth it to lose everything I've worked for if I just got busted again.

I wished I could get a job at one of those escort companies. Those girls are all prostitutes, anyway. But at least they get a real paycheck and they get to dress nice and they get to go out and dine with some nice guys. I wondered if any of those girls ever meet nice guys and get to dating them for real. I wondered if they ever fall in love with a nice guy who treats them right and they get married and have babies. I always wished I could work for one of those escort services, just for a little while, just until I could find a good man to fall in love with. I was just a hooker, but even that was just temporary.

I had enough money to get me a room for a

week at a small, dirty hotel. It was on the first floor, right next to the parking lot. It reminded me of the place I was staying when I was arrested. When I looked out my door, I could see a gated-off area where a pool used to be years ago. Now it was filled in with dirt and had a wooden picnic table on top of the mound.

I went down to the corner market for some groceries and cigarettes. I think one of the Muslims who ran the place was hitting on me, but he didn't seem like the kind of guy who was willing to pay for anything. He tried to tell me about his store being back open that day and that he thought I was pretty. That's all I understood. The rest just sounded like an old billy goat trying to talk to me. I tried to be nice to him and I nodded and smiled, and then I paid for my things and went back to my room around the corner. I thought about telling him how it works over here in America, that I would be more than happy to let him bend me over the counter if he'd be willing to pay for it like he would for a car wash or a haircut. I offer a service like anybody else, and all I expect is to get paid for my work. That dirty Muslim wouldn't be able to understand any of that, so I just went back to my room and made myself a sandwich and put my makeup on. An hour later, I was back in front of that corner store.

Three nights went by and I had nobody interested in me. Usually, I would move on and find another corner someplace else, but something made me stay put. Maybe it was the fear I felt that if I went to someplace busier, I would be picked up by another undercover cop. Or maybe it was that I never really wanted to turn tricks in the first place. I wanted a real job with a real paycheck. Most of all, I just wanted a family of my own. I wanted a good man who would treat me right, and I wanted a baby. All I wanted was a family.

By the end of the third night, I was ready to move on. I pushed myself into thinking that if I didn't turn at least one trick, I'd starve and not have enough money to pay the rent at the end of the week. I went back inside for a pack of cigarettes before starting my long walk to wherever I would end up.

There were a few other customers at the little store, but not many. There was this crippled guy in a wheel chair, and I could feel his eyes on me as I paid for my stuff. Everybody always stared at me. Either they wanted to fuck me, or they were silently condemning me for selling my ass on the street. Either way, if he wasn't asking for it, I wasn't going to advertise it any more than I already was with my hooker uniform, which I thought was small enough to fit my teenage daughter, if I ever had one.

Fuck! If I ever caught my daughter wearing something like this ...

Anyway, the crippled guy never said a word,

but I could feel his stare as he undressed me in his mind. If he'd ever gotten a piece before, it was never with a broad as hot as me, unless he paid for it, and *that* wouldn't have been cheap. The Muslims never said a word, neither. They just drooled as they stared at my tits. I counted my change back to myself and went outside for a quick smoke before I moved on, sure to pick up a client somewhere along the way, thus getting me back into the life that I swore to myself a million times that I'd leave behind forever.

As I tried to light my cigarette, I saw him drive his wheelchair out the door. He stopped, looked both ways, and sat still a while. It looked like he was lost and was trying to remember his way home. I wondered if he even had a home. He looked too clean to be homeless, but I couldn't imagine what kind of woman in her right mind would settle down with some guy with no legs.

Was he a war veteran? What war would that have been? He couldn't have been too much older than me, so he couldn't have lost them legs in a war. Maybe he was born that way. Either way, what kind of woman in her right mind would settle for a guy with no legs? But then again, I thought, what kind of woman in her right mind would turn herself into a hooker? I'm already a hooker, I reasoned, so why wouldn't I settle for a guy with no legs? I'm obviously not in my right mind, and from the waist up, he was kinda cute.

He tucked the bottle he just bought down at his side and he lit up his cigarette. His confident attitude almost gave him the appearance of a young Marlon Brando, except Brando was taller and had a cleaner shave. About that time is when I noticed that my lighter was empty.

"Excuse me, sir," I said as I stepped toward him from the wall. I must have scared him a little because he jumped a bit. "My lighter's out of gas. Can I borrow yours?"

He didn't respond with words, but he held out his lighter and struck the flame. As I leaned into it, I could feel his hands shaking. I couldn't tell if he was nervous because a girl had actually given him the time of day, or if it was because he was embarrassed to be associating with a prostitute.

I still couldn't tell which guy he was — the pervert or the preacher. Maybe I could play off like I am not a hooker at all, I thought, like I am just a girl who happens to be out after dark to buy some smokes. But would that work? I am, after all, wearing my hooker uniform. I might as well have had "hooker" sewn into the left breast corner of my shirt, and "Jenna" sewn into the right. These were my work clothes and I was still on the clock.

Fuck it. It was time for a break.

I tried to make small talk with him. I told him my name and pried his out of him: Arthur Boudreau. What was that, Italian? Great cooks, even better lovers. It really didn't matter, though.

"Where are you from?" I asked.

"San Antonio," he replied, like it was a dumb question. Maybe it was a dumb question, or maybe I just worded it wrong.

Maybe if he lived close — and alone — we could go back to his place and maybe watch some television. By now he was no longer a potential client, but maybe a potential friend. I don't know how that reasoning came into my mind, but why not? We both needed a friend. And besides, a guy with no legs couldn't kick me in the stomach like some guys do to their women. He'd never complain about me because he knows that he could never do any better than me. And I could never do any better than him. And he seems like a nice guy so far, I thought.

"No, I mean where do you live?" I rephrased my question. "Where's your house? Do you live around here?"

"No, it's a way's away," he told me, sounding almost embarrassed. "It's pretty far."

"Well, where are you headed?"

"Nowhere, really," he said, like he really meant that he was headed *nowhere*.

"Me, too." I tried to sound friendly, and for me I had to really try hard. Years of being stomped on and lied to by guys made me not a friendly person by nature. But I tried my best to be Arthur's friend. "My place is just right around the corner. If you'd like to have a drink, I'm sure we could find something good on the television.

Besides, it's getting cold out here and I have the heater already running there."

He didn't answer, but I could see in his eyes that he considered it, or at least wondered about it. So I slowly started walking back, and after a few steps, I stopped and looked back over my shoulder at him just as he began to follow.

The conversation during our walk was basically none at all. I asked him if he was married, and he just shook his head. It seemed like a sore subject. I figured that he was probably divorced. I decided to not ask any more questions about his family. What I really wanted to know was what happened to his legs, but I never developed the nerve to ask. Besides, if things went well between us, I figured it would come up eventually. He was probably some sort of war hero, and he probably didn't like talking about the war much.

I tried to not make it obvious, but I studied him hard. He was kinda scruffy, but with a clean shave, he'd be a really handsome guy. His arms were strong, so he probably worked out a lot. The only thing he lacked was the legs. And I could tell that he was smart, and overall, just a really good man.

I didn't drink very often at that time, so some of the details of what happened after we opened the bottle have since escaped me. But I do remember that he finally opened up to me and told me that he lived alone. He never married and hadn't had a girlfriend in quite some time. He had no kids and no other family to speak of except for his parents, but he said they weren't around anymore. I think he said they died, but I can't remember for sure. And he never told me about the war or about how he lost his legs.

One thing that I will never forget about him or that night was that he was extremely gentle and that we made love like it was the first time for both of us. It seemed to go on forever and when it was over, it seemed like it hadn't lasted long enough. Afterward, we just laid there awake, not saying a word, and I just fell asleep in his muscular arms.

And when I awoke in the morning, he was gone.

CHAPTER THREE:
THE WISDOM OF A PRIEST

A man in my congregation was robbed at gunpoint in New York. John was on vacation with his family and stopped at an old church in a historic part of the city. While his family was gazing at a large, beautiful fountain in the park across the street from the church, John found himself captivated by the majesty of the old church's tall bell tower. Not knowing what drew him to the structure, John soon found himself climbing the stairs to the top of the stone tower. Once at the top, John put his hand to the metal bell, and imagined how it has signaled the beginning of church services every Sunday for more than a hundred years. Then he turned to catch a glimpse of the magnificent city skyline.

John looked out to the far right and saw the skyscrapers in the distance. He saw his family across the street, still admiring the beautiful fountain in the center of the park. Then John noticed a man with a gun, just below the tower, robbing an elderly couple of their wallets. John looked out to his family and hoped they wouldn't decide to cross the street and, in turn, put themselves in harm's way. His heart was racing, and from several hundred feet away from where the sinister man stood, John was afraid.

After robbing the first couple, the young man with the gun simply turned and stopped another man while the elderly pair quietly walked away, no doubt thankful to still be breathing. And after the second man was robbed, he also simply walked away. Nobody made a big fuss over being robbed by a man with a gun, and nobody went to call the police. Maybe they were too scared. Either way, when John looked back to the gunman, he noticed the criminal looking up, right back into John's eyes. Then the man started walking toward the base of the tower.

John made the decision to run down the stairs, knocking into the robber on his way down. And when he'd reached the bottom, he'd just keep on running until he caught up with his family, and they'd all run together to the nearest telephone and call the police.

But what if the robber was to overpower him in the stairwell? What if he was to shoot John and simply be on his way? If the thick walls of the tower were to muffle the sound of the shot, it might be some time before his family stopped waiting for him to return and went up the stairs to find him. The last thing he wanted was for his family to see his bloody corpse sprawled across the stairs.

John abandoned the idea of running and thought of hiding, then taking the man by surprise and fighting him for the gun. But John had never been in a real fight before, let alone one fought for his own life against a hardened criminal. He would never be able to take the gun away from the young man, and death at the top of the tower was no more an ideal option than death in the stairwell.

In the end, John decided to ask God for the answer and prayed for a quick response. When John received no answer from God, he did the only thing he could think of to do, which was to crawl into the furthest corner, sit with his back to the wall and his knees to his face, and begin to shake uncontrollably.

As he heard the gunman's footsteps coming closer, John took the money from his wallet and hid it in one of his sock. The footsteps kept coming closer and closer, until John finally saw the man's feet appear at the top of the stairs. John never lifted his head any higher than the man's knees, but still he saw the shiny barrel of the gun. Without any prompting from the robber, John took the money back out of his sock and slowly reached it out to the man, who took the wad of cash and casually turned away and walked back down the stairs.

After what must have been at least fifteen minutes, John stood up and tried to regain control of his shaking body. He checked to make sure his fear had not caused him to wet himself. Then he looked out and noticed his family snapping photos of the fountain across the street, just as they had been before this whole incident ever started. He looked around for the young man with the big gun, but there was no trace of him. The criminal had simply vanished into the city, no doubt continuing to make money the only way he knew how.

When the family returned home after their vacation, John paid me a visit and told me the story. Then he asked me why God hadn't protected him and the other people from the crazed mugger. And why, even from the highest point in one of God's own churches, had God ignored his prayers?

I was still a young man then and very new to the church, but I knew that my position alone would validate any explanation I would give to him.

"God was listening," I told John. "It was both a scary and exciting ordeal for you, so maybe you just couldn't hear God's answer, but He was telling you to hand over your money to the man, and in doing so, nobody was harmed. God has a plan for everything that happens to each and every one of us, and, believe it or not, God even meant for that man to rob you."

"But why would God do *that*?" John asked in amazement of the simplicity of my answer.

"To teach you something very important," I responded.

"And what was he teaching me?" Now John was just confused.

"That, my son, is something you'll just have to figure out on your own."

How the hell was I supposed to know what God was saying? People think that just because I wear a white collar and constantly read from the bible, I have all the answers. The real answer, the one I *wanted* to tell him, is that some people are just messed up in their head. Some people are just lazy heathens who rob other people at gunpoint. But that's not what I was taught, so that's not what I teach.

But my answer seemed to comfort John, at least a little bit.

I don't recall what my childhood dreams ever were. I mean, some kids want to be professional baseball players, some want to be astronauts, but for as far back as I remember, I've always wanted to serve God. I'm sure I had some other profession in mind when I was a small child, but I honestly don't remember what it could've been. It would be easy to say that I knew from the day I was born that I would grow up to be a Catholic priest, but that it isn't exactly true.

I found my true calling when I was seventeen years old and my left wrist was cuffed to a chair in the local police department. I had been arrested and charged with stealing a very large sum of money. It was an unfortunate turn of events, but one that led me to the metaphorical fork in the road, and because I chose the direction I did, I was put on a straight and narrow path. And on my path are several others like me, those who chose the same direction I chose, those who chose the rocky road to salvation, rather than the easy road to Hell.

As a teenager, I volunteered at a church-run organization that took on the mission of rebuilding a large, old home to be used as a safe haven for abused and neglected children in the community. It was a tremendous effort that took most of my free time during the summer off from school. The rest of my free time was spent as a mentor for Ricardo, a local boy who was going down the wrong path.

When I spent time with Ricardo, we'd usually play basketball or watch television or I'd help him with his homework. I basically just tried to keep him out of trouble and provide him with positive influences as a responsible role model. And it was because of my association with Ricardo that I found myself cuffed to that chair.

One day, while I was on my way out to the project home site in my father's car, Ricardo popped up from the back seat. I don't know how I was able to maintain control of the car through all of the panic and fear that I initially felt before I realized who my uninvited passenger was.

"I'm sorry, but I just wanted to come along," Ricardo hurriedly explained, surely sensing my utter anger in his surprising me while I was driving on the freeway. "I knew if I asked you, you wouldn't let me go, but I just wanted to come along and help."

And he was right. He wasn't old enough or big enough to help with the actual construction of the house, but realizing I was now very close to the project site and very far from our own neighborhood, I allowed Ricardo to continue along. I'd just talk to the project supervisor once we got to the site, explain the situation, and ask if Ricardo could clean tools or hand out water to the volunteers. But first we had to make a stop at the convenience store just around the corner from the project house.

While I was buying sodas for the both of us, Ricardo disappeared into the back of the store. After I finished paying, I looked around for Ricardo and noticed his ball cap in the rear corner of the small store. When I met him back there, he was in the process of withdrawing money from a free-standing ATM along the back wall.

"It's my father's card," he explained as I approached. "He wanted me to bring him back some cash so he could go to the grocery store later on tonight."

"Well, alright, but we have to get going now." With a hand on his shoulder, I led him away from the machine.

"Wait," he said, turning back toward the machine. "The money didn't come out yet."

As I turned back to the machine, several bills slid out from the slit in the front of the ATM. I grabbed the stack and shoved them into Ricardo's hand. He pocketed the money and we headed out the door.

Several hours later, just as we were all cleaning and loading up the tools for the night, two police cars stopped in front of the house. An officer stepped out from one of the cars and approached a pair of volunteers and showed them a piece of paper. Everyone looked in my direction as one of the volunteers pointed at me, and the policeman started walking my way.

"Is this you?" He pointed to one of the two photos printed on the piece of paper.

"Yes, sir," I replied.

"Where's your buddy?" he asked, pointing to the second photo, the one of Ricardo.

"Ricardo?" All I was thinking about was that boy's bad reputation, and how I might now have a bad reputation because of him. I looked over to the area of the yard where Ricardo was hosing off some shovels used earlier in the day. The police officer followed my eyes to Ricardo, and with his firm grip around my left elbow, we were both hurrying over to the boy.

"Ricardo, is it?" the cop asked as we approached.

I was almost expecting Ricardo to spray the cop in the face with the hose and make a run for it. Instead, Ricardo just reached over and calmly turned off the hose.

"Yes, sir," Ricardo finally said after glancing up to his photo on the piece of paper the policeman held up.

"Well, I'm afraid the both of you are gonna have to come down to the police station to answer some questions," the officer explained. "But before we go, I'm gonna place you both under arrest."

Ricardo and I were cuffed together by our wrists and led to the first patrol car.

When we arrived at the police station, we were separated and put into different rooms for questioning. As it was explained to me, the photos were obtained from a camera on the ATM in the convenience store we stopped at. The card used to make the transaction was stolen, and after the large withdrawal had been made, the issuing bank called the card's rightful owner and inquired about it as a safety measure. The card's owner said he had not made the transaction and noticed his card was missing. Both he and the bank called the local police department, who obtained the photos from the ATM and our whereabouts from the store clerk, who I had previously mentioned the project home right around the corner to.

The cops were convinced I was the criminal mastermind who conned a young boy into stealing the money while I distracted the store clerk. They wrote out the statement, and Ricardo signed it in the presence of his father. By the time my parents arrived, the officers had already taken my finger prints and demanded a full confession. They figured Ricardo was too young to get any sort of conviction, but I was old enough to be tried as an adult, and that was what they planned to do to me.

My parents were unable to persuade the cops to let me go. They'd have to wait until I could be seen by the judge the next day to find out what would happen to me. In desperation, they called Father Michael Prienta, our priest.

When Father Prienta arrived, bible in hand, he was very angry. I couldn't hear what he was saying through the thick glass window that separated the main area of the police department from the tiny room I sat in with my parents, but I could tell that he was not happy. After he had said what he wanted to say, Father Prienta turned around and walked out the door. He hadn't come in to say anything to me or my parents, nor was he going to listen to anything the police officers had to say. He had simply turned around and walked out of the building. As soon as the door closed behind the angry priest, the police officer who brought me in hurried into the interrogation room and unlocked the handcuff around my wrist.

"We've decided to drop all the charges," he said, his eyes never leaving the floor. "All of the stolen money was retrieved, so there was no real harm done, I guess. Folks, you and your son are free to go."

Not waiting for him to change his mind, we all walked out and straight to my parents' car. I never saw Ricardo again and the whole situation was never spoken of by my parents or my priest, but I did have to fill in everyone at the project home who witnessed me being put into the squad car.

Though I am sure some small details have been skewed by age, one memory of that day has never been marred by the hands of time. It's my recollection of the power that made it possible for me to walk freely from that jail house after just a few short words from the neighborhood priest. That display of authority made me want to wear that white collar and help others in their times of pain and trouble. I wanted what Father Prienta had. I wanted that power.

After divinity school, I was assigned to a church in San Antonio, right there in the middle of all those military bases. A large number of those who attended were retired military men and their families who stayed in the local area after they'd left the active ranks of the Army and Air Force. Being new to the church, and even to the area, I made every attempt possible to get to know the people I spoke to every Sunday from the front of the church, and nearly everyone was glad to come up, introduce themselves and tell me something about their families. This was certainly the case with the Boudreau family.

David Boudreau was working on retiring from the Air Force when I first met him, and I would eventually see him retire and move with his wife out of the state in later years. Sarah was a stay-at-home mother. From our talks, I learned that she had always wanted to be a school teacher, but the constant moving the military required of her husband made it impossible for her to be anywhere long enough to begin a teaching career. That's why Mr. Boudreau took a position teaching new pilots. He knew it would keep them in San Antonio, with little possibility of the family having to relocate before the lieutenant colonel could retire in a few short years. But by the time they settled here, Sarah felt she was too old to start a new career, so she never joined the working community. Besides, she enjoyed the time she spent making a nice home for her family. I developed a friendship with the Boudreau family, a friendship that allowed me to help the family grow spiritually, as well as help shape myself into a wiser spiritual leader.

Most people who start on a fresh career path make goals for themselves. Priests are no different. My goal — however unoriginal it may have been for a young priest — was to look for that one person who had lost touch with God, the one who no longer felt the love of his maker, and do whatever I possibly could to bring that person back. I knew from my own experiences with other people that once a sheep has strayed away from the flock, it's hard to show him that he was on the right path to begin with, and if he continues down his own dark path, he may meet up with a wolf. And by that time, he will be alone and scared, and he will be too far from the flock to run back. This is a hard lesson to teach. Men don't like to be compared to sheep, a dumb animal. And metaphorically speaking, sheep who stray often don't really have a strong belief in wolves.

As it would later turn out, my sheep would be the son of David and Sarah Boudreau. But for now, Arthur Boudreau was a bright, young boy with a promising future. A little cocky at times, Arthur was still one of the nicest boys in the church. And he was intelligent, which is a trait passed down from his mother. From his father, however, Arthur received the heart of a true patriot.

In high school, the star basketball player was offered a full athletic scholarship, but he turned it down after much consideration. A basketball scholarship was a wonderful surprise he had never even thought to hope for, and something most young men would give anything to receive. But Arthur had always dreamed of a life serving his country, flying fighter jets in the Air Force, just as his father had done before him. And though getting a college degree from the military would cost Arthur nothing monetarily, it would come with an obligation to be commissioned into military service. He and I talked it over at great lengths, and in the end, I believe he made the right decision. Hard work and sacrifice could only make a man stronger, and the pride earned after unselfish dedication is more than could be understood by the average college student.

Arthur's decision to choose military service over the endless party of college life said a great deal about the young man's character, but it ultimately had no impact on his future. A traffic accident near the end of his senior year of high school left the boy in a wheelchair. Both of his legs had to be amputated right around the knees. He was in a coma for a couple of days, and when he awoke, he was in good spirits. I believe that was due to the realization of what had happened not yet setting in, and because of the high amount of medication flowing through the boy's veins. I tried to speak to him, but he didn't seem to understand everything I was saying.

I decided to give him some time to heal a little bit physically before I returned to help him emotionally and spiritually. I waited two days after I initially visited him the day he awoke, and returned to his hospital room. After I knocked, he began to yell obscenities, which basically said, "Get out!" I cautiously pushed the door open slowly, and immediately felt the impact of a flower vase shattering against the other side. And then there were more obscenities. Still with great caution, I continued into the room, figuring he assumed I was a nurse coming to give him more medication or touch his legs. If he knew it was me, he'd welcome me in and we'd talk together. I was wrong.

Seeing me standing there in my crisp black shirt and bright white collar, holding my bible, only made matters worse. He threw more obscenities my way, along with another flower vase. That one actually caught the side of my head a little bit, causing a minor gash that would leave a superficial but noticeable scar above my left eyebrow. I couldn't believe the nice, young man I had grown fond of recently could actually harm a priest intentionally.

His parents couldn't take it, either. They never had to deal with anything other than a perfect child before, and Arthur scared them now. I believe they gave up on him too soon, but I guess it's hard to understand the trauma experienced by a parent in a situation like that. Every time they visited him, they ran away a few minutes later in tears. He told them not to come around anymore.

I think he blamed his father for the traffic accident, and that basically set the tone for their relationship. Arthur also gave orders to allow no other visitors, which included his friends from school and myself. Being a priest has its privileges, though, and the hospital staff was more than happy to bend the rules and allow me to enter his room. They figured I might be the only person who could control Arthur. I'd like to say I helped out, but that just simply isn't true. He had closed his eyes and ears to God and the rest of the world, and what he really needed, I figured, was time.

By the time he was released from the hospital, the school year was over and Arthur had no diploma. Nor did he have any of his old friends, who he never allowed to visit after the accident.

While in the hospital, Arthur turned eighteen. His parents came by with a small cake, but no one ate any of it. They didn't bring any presents for him because they didn't know what to get for him. Sporting goods were out of the question, as were new clothes. They just brought the cake and watched the television with him in his hospital room. I came by later, and we watched even more television. He never spoke a word to any of us that day. And he never spoke much at all to anyone after that.

He did convince me, though, to help him move out of his parents' house and into an apartment of his own. Whatever insurance checks and disability benefits he was entitled to would be enough to cover rent and food and all the utilities. He wanted to live independently. He'd be alone, but at least he'd be independent.

As my "lost sheep," he never failed to challenge my dedication, but I must admit that I almost lost hope at times. I would visit him often and deliver him a condensed version of my weekly sermon, but even that was too much for him to take. He often told me that he had no time to listen to made-up stories about God, and often told me to leave his apartment, which I rarely did at his request. I could see that he was through with God, but that he was also in need of a friend. Besides, he was still rather strong physically, and stronger mentally than anyone I have ever met. If he really wanted me gone from his home, he would have removed me himself.

After a while, I came over so often that I didn't bother to knock. Again, if he really didn't want me there, he would have locked the door. Or maybe he knew it would be pointless since I had made myself a copy of the key to his front door. Either way, I'd come over and talk, or just sit and watch the television for a while. And I made sure he always had enough groceries and a holiday meal. He stopped asking me why I did what I did, because he always knew that my answer would relate to God. And I'm sure that deep down inside, he actually enjoyed the company, even when no words were spoken by either of us during an entire visit.

And this went on for years. His parents sold their house and moved to a retirement community somewhere in Florida. Arthur never had a phone in his apartment because he despised hearing them ring. After several unanswered letters, his parents stopped writing to him anymore. He had cut himself off from any family he had left in the world. He pretended that it was how he wanted it to be, but his stubbornness was too thin to mask his pain and loneliness. That's when he really began to drink heavily.

Back at the church, I saw families come and go. Everything was constantly changing. In ten years, there were very few people in the congregation who were there to see my first days with the church. And of those who had been there all along, I am sure even very few of them could remember David and Sarah Boudreau, let alone their young son who stopped attending Sunday services all those years ago.

But one day, he came back. He showed up and sat in the back of the church for the entire service, and then he was the first one out the door. He didn't come again for several weeks, and I didn't push the issue. I thought that his showing up at all was promising, and I didn't want to push him away again by being what he might have perceived as pushy. And then he finally came back about a month or so later, hiding in the confession booth. He wasn't really there to confess, but to make a mockery of God and me. I said some very strong things to him in hopes that he would snap out of the self-pity that still tortures him every day.

It may have been the wrong thing for me to do, but I felt that I was out of options. He left in a hurry, and I didn't see him again for probably close to a year. That's when he showed up and begged me to help him, because he had nobody else to turn to in his dire situation. It seems that he had gotten himself into some trouble and needed some guidance.

I spared him the lecturing. He knew that what he had done was wrong and that he now had to face the consequences. I told him that I would help him in any way I could, and in the end, that meant asking the church to hire an attorney to help one of its members.

PART TWO

DR. J. OLIVER JOHNSON

CHAPTER FOUR:
BEGINNINGS OF A NEW MOTHER

I pissed on the stick and waited ten minutes. Then the fucking thing changed colors. I don't remember if it went to pink or blue or piss-yellow, but I fumbled for the box and matched the color with what it meant. I was fucking pregnant.

In my profession, you can't be too sure who the daddy is when you wind up with a baby in your belly. It could have been any guy with correct change and a few free minutes.

After going to the free clinic and figuring out how far along the baby was, I counted back and tried to estimate a conception date. It wasn't hard for me to figure out the exact day and who the father was to this bastard inside me. There was only one guy in the past six months or so who got to ride bare-back. It was that goddamn legless shit. He's the one that ruined me.

A simple procedure would snatch this baby out of me before it ever starts growing, but that ain't a service offered at that free clinic, and I sure as hell couldn't afford to pay a real doctor to do it. Maybe I'd get lucky, I thought, and some drunk cowboy would kick me in the ribs hard enough to send the kid oozing down my inner thigh. I'd simply flush the toilet and walk away. Problem solved.

The free clinic did, however, provide all pregnancy services free of charge. They'd make sure my baby was healthy and safe and they'd help me during the birthing process and everything. They'd give me plenty of vitamins and medicines and I could deliver the healthiest baby ever.

I should've been happy, I told myself. There are people out there who can't have kids on account of some medical problem they have. They pray to God in vain for years just for a baby of their own, and here I am praying I didn't have this one coming. So maybe one of *them* would pay me for *my* baby.

First things first, I had to quit smoking and drinking. In the beginning, I just switched to light cigarettes and light beer, but the doctors at the free clinic said that it wasn't good enough and I had to quit all together. They also said I had to quit whoring, but I still had bills to pay. So I just raised my rates and increased the level of pleasure

I gave to my clients. It meant lowering my standards and forgetting any morals I still had left, but it also meant turning less tricks each night. And that, I figured, was safer for my baby.

As I got further along in the pregnancy, I thought I'd have a decline in business, but that just wasn't the case. You wouldn't believe how many guys get off on banging some pregnant bitch, just so long as she wasn't his wife. I was generally just on my back the whole time, anyway, so it wasn't like it was any more work on my part. But the guys just loved giving it to a skinny girl with a huge gut.

After I was pretty far along in the pregnancy, I was informed by the nurse at the free clinic that selling my baby for adoption was illegal and would never happen. That's when I decided to go ahead with the abortion. I saved up every dollar I made and when I had enough, I went to one of them women's clinics that take care of abortions on the side. But they said that the pregnancy was too far along for me to have it taken out, so I'd have to go ahead and deliver it as planned. I was gonna be stuck with this fucking baby and there wasn't anything that could be done about it.

What the hell did I know about babies? I knew that I couldn't afford one on my salary, even on my best night. This baby needed a father and a better life than I could provide on my own.

I ruled out getting a new boyfriend. No decent man would take in a pregnant hooker and then raise the baby like it was his own. I needed to go back to the source of this problem. I needed to find that legless shit.

I tried for a week to remember his name. And then it just popped into my head: Arthur Boudreau. Ah, yes, the Italian war hero. He was partial to bourbon whiskey, if I remembered correctly. He was a bit odd, but that was probably due to getting his legs blown off by a land mine or something. He still seemed like a nice guy, and he seemed to have taken a liking to me that one night. And besides, when would he have another chance at a real life, one with a devoted woman and a beautiful child? No other woman would give him the time of day, let alone offer to move in with him and give him any offspring. I was sure he'd answer the phone and be glad when I told him who it was that was calling him.

"I was wondering what ever happened to you," he'd say. "I've thought about you every day since that night we fell in love."

"Me, too," I'd cry into the phone. "And, honey, I'm having your baby."

Then he'd come get me and take me back to his house and we'd turn the spare bedroom into a nursery and I'd cook him dinner and he'd hold me every night before we fell asleep.

But unfortunately, his name wasn't listed in the phonebook. I tried every spelling variation I could think of for Boudreau, but the only listing was for a David Boudreau. I called it and some

Mexican answered the phone. When I asked for Arthur Boudreau, he said, "Boudreau don't live here no more." And then he hung up the phone.

And that was that.

When the baby was finally born, it was the worst day of my life. The doctors wouldn't let me eat the entire day, and the pain medications weren't doing a fucking thing to make the hurt go away. When it finally came out, I passed out as they were sewing me back up. I never got to hold my baby until later on that night. That's when I found out it was a boy.

"What are you gonna name him?" one of the nurses asked as she was preparing to hand him over to me for the first time. The truth is that I never considered what to name him before that exact moment. I probably shouldn't give him my last name, or else people would think he was fathered by my own daddy or one of my brothers. If this would have happened a few years back, I wouldn't have been surprised to have a baby by one of those dirty pigs. But this baby had his own daddy, even though his daddy didn't know it yet.

"Boudreau," I said. "His name is Arthur Boudreau, Junior."

"Well, that's a fine name," she answered back to me as she slid the baby into my arms.

Yes, it was a fine name, indeed. And though I was positive of the names when I went to write them down for the birth certificate, I misspelled his first name with an *er* at the end instead of the *ur* his daddy used. And what's worse is that I never knew what his daddy's middle name was, so our baby son just went without one.

I had always hoped to find Arthur one day, and when he saw me and our baby and took the both of us in, the boy would take his daddy's middle name and truly be his father's son. Of course, as I later found out, I'd have to also change the spelling of his first name. It was a simple mistake.

Life got really hectic after I went home from the hospital. The crying baby needed to be fed all the time, and it shit more than any animal I've ever had as a pet. Those disposable diapers were more expensive than my meals for an entire week, so I took to making some diapers out of old shirts and blankets. I couldn't leave the baby alone long enough to walk the streets all night like I was used to. I could only leave it there long enough to go pick up a client and bring him back to the hotel room. And most guys found an infant baby crying from behind the bathroom door to be a distraction, and my income certainly reflected it.

The stretch marks and extra skin I got from having that bastard inside of me for almost nine months didn't do much for my business, either. Them celebrities I see on the television while I try to get the kid to sleep always showed women who had the same bodies they had when they were in high school, even after they delivered a child into the world. Fuck 'em, I'd say. It sure must be nice to not have to work every day and just go to the gym and have surgery to fix it all. If I had that kind of money, I sure as hell wouldn't look the way I do, and I sure as hell wouldn't be no whore.

My life was once again going down the shitter and there wasn't anything I could do about it. I thought about places where I could leave the baby so someone could find it and give it a good home and I'd be rid of it. Then I'd have those motherly feelings that made me want to keep it for some reason. What I really needed was that crippled fuck that got me into this mess in the first place.

And then I saw him there one night. I thought it may have just been a hallucination on account that I hadn't eaten in almost two days. I was on my way to that little Muslim corner store just around the way from the hotel. I was hoping to bum a smoke or two from someone coming out of the store. What I found instead was my baby's daddy, looking as pathetic as he did the day he used me and left me there in that filthy hotel room.

"Hey, Arthur," I called out as we both approached the door to the little store. He looked up and stopped his chair right there in the middle of the sidewalk. Then he put his head down and kept on into the corner store. I caught up with him in the back of the store, picking out his favorite brand of whiskey. "Hey, Arthur. I've been looking for you for long time. Must've been at least a year now, right?"

"Oh, hi," he said, still not looking back up at me. "We must've just missed each other by a matter of minutes, probably. See, I still come in here all the time."

"Well, I'll be," I said to him. "I've been looking for you for a long time now. We have some stuff we gotta talk about."

I could almost see a little spark ignite in his eyes when I told him that I had been looking for him. I figured he probably hadn't gotten laid during that whole year and he often pined for that one piece of ass again. I decided to play along and not mention his baby just yet. Besides, if I did things right this time, maybe we'd all be going back to his house by the end of the night.

"Yeah, I've actually wondered what happened to you a couple of times," he said. His personality seemed a bit less shy now than when I saw him outside the store a minute earlier, and a hell of a lot less shy than he was when I first met him. I knew he wanted me to ask him back to my room.

"I still stay just right around the corner from here," I told him. "How'd you like to stop by for a little while? That is, unless you've got somewhere important to go."

"No, I'm not really headed anywhere tonight," he replied. "Sure, I can stop by for a few minutes, I guess. Just let me pay for this and I'll meet you outside."

We could both hear the baby crying from across the parking lot as we approached the door to my room, but neither of us said anything. Maybe he thought it came from next door, but when I opened up, the source of the screaming was unmistakable.

"You have a visitor tonight?" he asked. "Are you babysitting?

"No, sugar, he's mine," I explained though a forced smile. "He's just a few months old now."

Arthur's face turned as pale as a ghost as I'm sure he was doing the math in his head.

"Here, let me go get him real quick," I said as I ducked into the bathroom and came back with a smiling baby boy. "His name's Arthur Boudreau, Junior."

"Oh, fuck no!" he screamed, and he began moving his wheelchair backwards as fast as he could. "Oh, fuck no!"

I didn't know what reaction I was expecting him to have, but this sure as hell wasn't the one I was hoping for. I held out the baby toward him so he could get a better look. If he just saw how much they looked like each other, I was sure he'd fall in love with him and love the baby just as I did. I was hoping he'd be excited to have a son. Sure, he wouldn't be much as far as helping him work on his jump shot, but every man wants a son. If I knew nothing else about men, at least I knew that every man in the entire world wants a son to carry on his family name. And this ungrateful motherfucker just wanted to run away from it.

"I don't want no baby and I ain't having no baby!" he yelled as he fumbled with the door knob over his right shoulder.

"It's alright," I tried to assure him. "We'll do it together. You and me and our baby. We can be a family together."

"I don't want nothing to do with no hooker," he yelled back as the door finally started to open before being obstructed by the wheel of his chair.

"And *that's* why you followed me to my room, right?" I knew he still wanted to fuck me, just like he did last year. "That's why you came back again!"

"Fuck you, hooker," he growled back as he finally pulled the door all the way open and fumbled his way outside. "You keep that little shit to yourself. I ain't having no hooker's baby!"

"It's too late, Arthur Boudreau. I already know your name and you're gonna support this baby," I hollered across the parking lot from the edge of my room. "You're a daddy now and you'd better get your shit together, 'cause if you don't start paying for this here baby, the judge is gonna make you pay!"

I knew I didn't have any money for a real lawyer, but I heard that some of them help out poor people in trouble and they do it for free. It helps them look like decent people and it's probably just some sort of tax write-off for them, anyway.

I went the next day and looked for a lawyer downtown to take my case. I brought Junior on the bus with me 'cause I didn't know how long it would take, and I didn't want him sitting there alone all day in the hotel bathroom, just starving to death and marinating in his own piss and shit. That would be a hell of a mess to clean up when I got back home before I was able to go to bed. I just couldn't sleep at night with that damn baby crying like he does when he hasn't eaten all day and the smell of shit so strong it chokes me when I breathe in. Plus, I figured, I could really use the sympathy he'd bring me from the lawyers if I was gonna get one of them to represent me for free.

And then I found one who said he could get that crippled fuck to pay me a lot of money each month, and maybe even get me some of the military pension he had to be getting since he got his legs blown off fighting in whatever war he fought in. If I wasn't gonna have my baby's daddy to live with us and help take care of us, at least I'd have a little money help from him. And at least I'd always have my baby.

CHAPTER FIVE:
THE EMERGENCE OF A FATHER

I really thought that I'd never have to see that damned priest again, but there I was, begging him for his help.

I needed more than just some useless advice this time; I needed someone to tell me what I had to do, and most of all, guide me along the whole way. All Father Silva ever did was talk about what the bible says and what Jesus did when he was faced with a problem similar to mine. But I highly doubt Jesus ever got laid, let alone by a hooker. Unless that whore Mary Magdalene actually gave it up to him, but I don't remember that ever being written about in the bible. And from what I actually do remember from the bible, Jesus never faced a paternity suit.

"I'm going to be tough on you, Arthur," Father Silva said to me. "First of all, I'm going to have to tell you that I am very disappointed that you allowed yourself to get into this mess in the first place. But I guess that's what comes with never showing up to church, isn't it?"

"Please, father, don't lecture me, not now." If I wasn't going to get anything more than just a stern talk, I'd take my business elsewhere and handle this mess on my own. The freeway still called to me like the ghost of a woman who calls out to the puppy who strayed from her yard. It sounded sweet and comforting, like if I go back, I could come in out of the cold rain. But as soon as the puppy comes back into the yard, he's beaten in the face by a switch the old bitch pulls from the tree in the yard, and the puppy is back on the chain.

If I went back to the freeway, I'd probably just fuck it up. I'd probably end up even more crippled than I am now, and I'd be unable to push myself back onto the freeway after that. Even if I never make it back there, I at least need to know that I am able to do so, if I ever get the courage up.

"Alright then," Father Silva continued. "Just as long as you know how I feel."

"If I would've known she got pregnant, I would've made that bitch get an abortion," I explained. "I would've spent the money, no questions asked. It would've saved me a lot more money in the long run."

"You shut up!" Father Silva snapped at me. "First of all, you watch your language in here. This isn't a bar or a brothel. And second, you stop talking that trash about abortions and saving money. This baby is a living child, and if I am to help you through this mess, you'll not be forgetting that this child deserves to breathe and live just as much as you do."

I was about to explain to him that I never considered myself worthy of breathing, but figured it best to just keep my mouth shut. It would only piss him off even more, and he was the only person who could help me out. If he turned me away, it would be the freeway tonight, for sure.

"I'm sorry, father," I said, and it was the first time in a long while that I actually meant it.

"Alright then," he continued. "The next thing you're going to have to do is start acting like a man. Whether or not you wanted to be one, you are now a father, and you have to act like it. Quit all that whining, lift your head up high and stand up straight."

He then paused and looked down at me, probably expecting me to explain to him that standing at all is impossible for me, but I didn't say anything. I knew what he meant, even though I wasn't sure if I could change myself into this man he said I needed to be — or even if I *wanted* to be this man.

"You've lived your whole life as a victim," he began his lecture. "You've cried and whined whenever the world didn't go exactly as you planned it. You fell out of a truck and lost your legs and you blamed God. You refuse to work and you spend all of your free money on alcohol, but still you blame the government for your being penniless. You're a bitter, angry fool, yet you drink yourself to sleep and blame society because you're lonely."

"But none of that is my fault," I tried to explain.

"I said to shut up and listen," he interrupted. "From what you've told me, this girl wants you to have a family with her and your baby. Well, she obviously saw something in you that nobody else can see. She saw a man with potential, and you ignored her. Sure, she's a prostitute, but Rudolph Nureyev was gay, and you can't tell me that he wasn't the absolute best at what he did. He was very well-known for mastering all the best moves."

"Gay moves?" I wondered out loud. "Who the fuck is Rudolph Nureyev?"

"No, dance moves," Father Silva corrected. "He was a ballet dancer."

"Here in San Antonio?"

"No, he's not an American."

"Russian?" I quizzed.

"I don't know. Maybe"

"But I thought all Russians were atheists."

"That's not the point," the priest barked at me. "The point is, he's a sinner, just like the rest of us, and he's still a highly respected man throughout the entire world. Maybe it was a bad example, but my point is that we are all flawed. Some people's flaws are just more obvious than others."

"I think you've lost me, father."

"Nureyev was a great dancer and people respect him, despite the fact that he's gay, and therefore a sinner. This woman made you happy at one time and you even had feelings for her. And now you can't say a single nice thing about her because you can't get over the fact that she's a prostitute. And let me remind you, my son, that you're no angel."

"Yeah," I agreed. "Those who seek pleasure in glass whore houses shouldn't throw stones, right?"

"Something like that," he said, with almost a faint trace of a smile.

"So, what are you saying I should do? You want me to marry her and move her and the baby into my apartment?"

"Oh, hell no," he shot back. "You aren't going to have some hooker moving in and taking over your life. You would be worse off than you are now if you let that woman into your home. All she wants is your money."

"But I don't have any money," I said.

"She obviously doesn't know that," he explained. "But if a judge says you have to pay her child support, you're going to have to get a job and pay that woman her child support. The baby is yours, and you're responsible for helping to provide him food, shelter, medicine and anything else he needs for the next eighteen years. I know you don't want to be a father right now, but you also can't leave that baby in that woman's care."

"Well, what are you suggesting I do?"

"The church has a lawyer," he started.

"Oh, just in case some little boy says you touched him in his holey place?"

"I said to shut up." He seemed pretty angry at that one, but he continued anyway. "We have a church lawyer, and I'm sure it wouldn't take too much of an arm-twisting to convince him to take on your case pro bono. And if not, I'm sure the church could take care of the bill, just as long as you're a member of the church. Either way, you'll have a lawyer to guide you through all the legal hurdles."

"Thank you, father."

"But he isn't going to just make this woman and child disappear from your life," he continued. "He's going to ask that you at least get partial custody of the child."

"But I don't *want* partial custody of the child."

"Let me put it a different way for you," he said. "If she gets full custody, you'll be paying her a lot of child support. If you share custody, you'll either be paying a little bit of child support or maybe even none at all."

"But that means that I'll have to take care of it, right?"

"Yes, sometimes, but you can do it. It's really not that hard. And if you need help, I will be there to assist you. And there are plenty of church members who are also experienced mothers and fathers who would be more than happy to help you out from time to time. We even have free child care on certain nights here at the church, so we'd be able to give you a break every now and then."

"But if I'm going to take this kid, just to pass the responsibility on to you and the church and anybody else who's willing to help, then what's the point of taking over custody?"

"Because you will help raise him. He needs his father, because it's apparent that his mother isn't much of a mother at all. You *will* raise this child," he demanded. "That's my terms. Do you want my help or not?"

After several minutes of silence, I agreed to the whole deal. I would agree to let this lawyer take my case free of charge and agree to do whatever else is suggested by Father Silva or the lawyer. I promised to raise the baby to the best of my ability and to not let my pride stand in the way of my asking for help whenever it all got to be too much for me. I also gave Father Silva my word that I would try my best to make it in to church every Sunday, and when the boy was in my custody, he'd also be coming.

"Don't worry, my son," Father Silva said through a smile after sealing our verbal contract. "God has a plan for each of us, and as long as we stick to this plan that we've just set for ourselves, everything will turn out for the best. I promise this to you."

Yeah, well fuck promises and fuck plans. I should have known better than to go against my own instincts to simply flee the state and leave my problems behind me. It should have been tattooed on my brain at that point that no course we ever mapped out would lead to a good conclusion. The best-laid plans of priests and cripples often go awry.

CHAPTER SIX:
THE GUIDANCE OF A PRIEST

Arthur Boudreau made a deal with the devil. And then he made a deal with me.

Satan gave Arthur everything he ever asked for, and then some. Arthur had his freedom, his independence, and Satan even granted Arthur the one thing he longed for the most. Arthur was given the means and the opportunity for the family he had always wanted. Arthur was shown the path to a loving young woman, though troubled as she was. With that woman, Arthur created a son, someone who he could help mold into a fine prodigy, someone who could be more successful than Arthur could ever be. And someone who Arthur could love and be proud of, as his son's accomplishments would also be reflections of the wisdom and teachings of his father. And Satan also gave Arthur the stubbornness and ignorance to pass all of this up in exchange for a life of self-pity and depression.

I was determined to right this wrong, to lead Arthur back away from Satan and into the love of God. Arthur was, in fact, my lost sheep, and just as a shepherd in the literal sense may very well know where his stray sheep has gone, it's still not the same as having him safe in the pasture of green grass with the rest of the flock. That was part of our deal. I agreed to bring him some satisfaction and relief, and he agreed to rejoin the flock.

Our lawyer, Mr. Spalding, agreed to take on the case pro bono. He was bound by contract to take on any case filed on behalf of or against the church, and I think he had been somewhat disappointed with the complete lack of scandal involving the church since he signed the contract several years earlier. I don't know if this was his reason for taking on Arthur's case or if he was sincerely concerned with helping out a fellow human being. Whatever his reason was, he agreed to help, and I believed he was very competent to do so.

When the case was brought into court, I could tell right away that things would go in our favor. The judge was typical of one you'd see in a movie that takes place in a courtroom setting. Judge Whittaker — his first name was something like Harland or Horace, something very stereotypical of a judge, I thought — was an older white-haired man, who I could tell was very conservative. I suppose that it didn't hurt that the mother of Arthur's baby had no friends or family to call upon as character references and Mr. Spalding had a priest at his disposal to vouch for Arthur's character and good intentions. In the end, I almost felt bad for the woman, as if we had blindsided her without giving her a chance to defend herself. But then I had to remember that it wasn't a petty quarrel between her and Arthur, but rather a fight for the well-being of their child.

Mr. Spalding did everything we had asked of him, and I believe he had done so with absolute professionalism. He requested partial custody of the boy for Arthur and said Arthur was willing to pay back-due child support costs, but asked that he not be held responsible for any future payments of such.

The judge, upon seeing the obvious flaws in both parents, requested all available records for both parties, which included police records, credit reports, proof of income and proof of residence.

Arthur had no police records. A life-long drunk as he was, he never drove anymore and so he was never arrested for drunk-driving. He had been at the same address for several years and had not one single disturbance call made to his residence by his neighbors. He usually drank alone in his apartment, so he never even allowed himself to get into any sort of altercation at a bar. Aside from his drinking, which he assured the judge was no longer a problem, Arthur appeared to be a model citizen.

But Jenna Carroll, the child's mother, had not such a clean slate. It seems she had numerous arrests and citations for prostitution, drug possession and petty theft. She had moved several times within the past few years, mostly from one hotel to another, and there were several gaps in time when she herself had no recollection as to where she had been living. And at that time, she and her baby were living in a room at a hotel that was very well known for being home to drug addicts, prostitutes and various other felons.

Income was another factor. Although Arthur had not been employed since he was a teenager, at least he had a permanent steady income. The checks he received relating to his accident made sure he would be able to support himself for life, as well as provide financial support for his son. He would never be wealthy by these means, but he and his son would also never starve. Records obtained from his apartment manager showed that he had not even been late with a single rent payment since becoming a resident of the building.

Ms. Carroll, however, had very little income. And what she could account for during the previous three years had only been from money received by the unemployment administration, which would not have been enough to live on. It seemed she made no attempt at finding employment and it was evident that she survived off of earnings made by her occupation as a prostitute.

After a week's worth of afternoons in the judge's chambers, Judge Whittaker came to his determination.

Arthur was told he would have to pay the back-due child support, as was expected, and that he would not be forced to pay any future payments to Ms. Carroll. Everything else the judge said, however, was totally unexpected. Ms. Carroll would retain absolutely no custody of her son, but would instead be granted supervised visitation rights. Instead of partial custody, Arthur was granted temporary full custody if he wanted it. If not, the child would be placed into foster care and Arthur would also be granted only visitation rights.

Judge Whittaker said Ms. Carroll had no business being a mother in the first place and said he believed Arthur would be a responsible parent if he really tried. He also said that he would not be able to give Arthur only partial custody if the child was to be put into foster care. "A child needs at least one real parent," he said, "not just a part-time babysitter."

I almost expected Arthur to flatly turn down

the chance to raise the boy. With the child in foster care, Arthur would be free to continue doing just as he pleased without the worry of caring for a crying baby. Either way, he'd be off the hook as far as paying any child support payments. But at the first glance I gave him after the judge offered him full custody, Arthur turned from me, stone-faced, and stared the judge squarely in the eyes.

"Yes, your honor," he said matter-of-factly. "Thank you, sir."

"Does this mean you want your son?" the judge asked. "Yes, sir, it does." And with that, Jenna Carroll began a frantic howl that I am sure was heard far beyond the walls of Judge Whittaker's chambers.

"You heartless bastard," she bellowed at the judge. "You can't give my baby to that freak. He doesn't even want him. I want my baby!"

It was the first time I think she saw her child as anything more than just a means of income by way of child support payments.

"You control yourself, ma'am," the judge demanded. "I'm ordering you both into counseling. And remember, Mr. Boudreau, that this is only temporary custody. You can keep your son only after proving that you can handle the responsibility. If you give this court any reason to doubt your abilities to be a parent, you won't be one."

Ms. Carroll went home empty-handed, except

for a check I insisted Arthur write out immediately for the back-due child support he owed her. Arthur went home with his son, and a mountain of doubt and worry.

Arthur had a tough time adjusting to life as a father. He actually took me up on my offer to stay with him through the night so I could help him care for the baby. The one night turned into three nights as I helped turn his bedroom into something that was more accommodating for a baby. Church members donated things like clothes, diapers, a crib and an old dresser, and I showed Arthur how to give the baby his bottles and change diapers and bathe the child. Since Arthur often fell asleep on the couch most nights, we rearranged his living room so it could double as his bedroom. It wasn't how most men would choose to live, but Arthur wasn't in a position that most men find themselves in.

After the second day, I noticed Arthur always referred to his son as "the boy" or "the baby." He never called him by his given name, Arther. Maybe it was because he felt strange about having something named for him, or maybe it was because the baby's name was officially misspelled. I told Arthur that eventually he'd have to start calling his son by a proper name.

"No, I don't believe I'll be calling him Little Art," he said.

"How about Junior?" I suggested.

"No, that's stupid, too," he grinned. "I think

I'll start calling him Dylan."

"As in Bob Dylan?"

"I've got all of Bob Dylan's albums playing all the time," he boasted. "At least this way I'll never forget what to call the boy."

It was true that Arthur had his Bob Dylan records constantly playing, but he didn't have every one of the man's albums. So when I was at the store looking for a few "how-to" baby guide books, I picked up the albums Arthur needed to complete his Bob Dylan catalogue, *Slow Train Coming* and *Saved*. I suppose Arthur had knowingly left these records out of his collection, but I figured the singer's faith-based albums might be able to speak to Arthur in a way I had not been able to. If Bob Dylan, a born Jew, could become a practicing Christian, maybe his spiritual music would be able to help get Arthur back on the road he needed to be following. Arthur actually played the albums, though I am not sure he was really listening to the messages in the songs.

Despite my guidance and help, Arthur still refused to go to church.

"It was part of our agreement," I told him, but he still resisted. "I helped you get your son, and you agreed to come to church."

"But I'm not ready to go yet," he whined. "And if I'm not ready to be there, it won't be productive and it'll only make me hate going even more."

"Oh, that's a load of crap and you know it," I countered. "If you don't have any better reason to go, you'll be sure to get some decent nap time in during my sermons. Maybe you'll subconsciously absorb some of what I say. Besides, there will be plenty of ladies there who'd be more than happy to hold Dylan during the service."

I figured that getting him in the door would be the end of the first battle. Dealing with Arthur was like dealing with a three-year-old child. When he's set in his ways, it's tough to break him free of his routines. But after telling him that I would sit there and preach to him until I was blue in the face, he reluctantly agreed to go.

Once we were there, I saw a side of Arthur I don't believe I had seen since he was a child himself. The ladies and young girls flocked to him and commented on the beautiful baby he held in his arms, and for the first time in a decade, I saw a little bit of pride in his eyes. I've heard stories that some men use children as a way to meet women to date, but Arthur had no such intentions in mind. I believe he actually liked the attention he received as a father, even though he didn't see himself as one.

"Yes, he's a big boy," he said when one woman commented on how healthy the baby looked. "And he's heavy, too. I'm gonna to have to replace the shocks on my wheelchair if he don't learn how to walk real soon."

Arthur got several offers by the women to watch Dylan, free of charge, if he ever needed a break.

"Oh, we just love kids," one elderly woman told him after the service. "Ours are all grown now, but we still have all their old toys sitting around collecting dust. You're welcome to have them if you want them. I sure miss having a baby around the house. You cherish the time you're still able to hold him. It won't last long."

I actually thought Arthur would feel insulted by the attention, as if he assumed they singled him out and pitied him because of his physical handicap. But I think he actually saw past that for once and began to feel the real joy of having a child of his own. I think it made him feel almost normal again. He accepted several phone numbers of potential babysitters and promised he'd bring Dylan back next Sunday.

The Boudreau family, Arthur and Dylan, attended church pretty regularly after that. Dylan's mother met with them on two separate occasions in a park near the church. A woman assigned by the court sat with Ms. Carroll on a park bench as the young mother held her baby son. I sat with Arthur from a distance and we just watched and conversed until the visit was over.

Ms. Carroll didn't make it out to the next scheduled visit, nor did she attend any counseling sessions. Arthur went to his sessions, though I don't know if they did any good for him. But still, he became what everyone would say was a great father to his son.

Arthur was called into court one more time when Dylan was about six months old. The court was unable to reach Ms. Carroll for a few months and decided to lift the temporary status on Arthur's custody of Dylan, believing him to be a fit and loving father.

I shared the same views as the court and was extremely proud of Arthur's recent responsible behavior. I also took pride in knowing that my actions brought this on and bettered the lives of Arthur and his son.

Arthur did drink from time to time, but I never associated it with his waning attendance in church over the next couple of years. He eventually got the hang of taking care of Dylan and even enrolled the boy in preschool, in which Dylan excelled beyond his peers. He was the first to learn to write his name and count to ten. I believe Arthur took pride in having a gifted child and helped him at home with his education.

Dylan's academic accomplishments furthered as he entered kindergarten, and he became one of the more popular kids in the school, earning admirers in both students and teachers alike. He was on the honor roll from the fourth grade all the way up to the eighth grade, and he always had a near-perfect attendance record.

He also attended Sunday school every week until he entered high school, and he always came to church services, with or without his father.

I doubt he ever really questioned his mother's absence from his life. Many families these days are of broken homes caused by the rising number of divorces every year. But I am sure Arthur filled his son in on certain details about the boy's mother and the first few months of his life.

Other than having a father who was without his legs, Dylan's upbringing was relatively normal by today's standards.

He grew up with hopes and dreams and he always did his best to make sure he accomplished everything he set out to do. I believe he had decided to become a school teacher, and that is what he pursued while taking courses at a local college. His father and I were both extremely proud of him.

DR. J. OLIVER JOHNSON

PART THREE

DR. J. OLIVER JOHNSON

CHAPTER SEVEN:
THE LOVE OF A YOUNG GIRL

I hate niggers. I've always hated niggers. And I don't mean to say that I hate all black people. I mean those black people who make all the negative stereotypes true.

I mean the guys who wear their pants sagging just below their asscracks. Those who don't want to work, but still complain that the racist government is keeping them poor and ignorant. Those who refuse to get an education because they're convinced they'll make a million dollars playing basketball or rapping about drugs, murdering cops and exploiting women.

And I am talking about the promiscuous girls

who get pregnant in high school, just because their promiscuous mothers got pregnant with them in high school. I mean the people who can't afford to take care of themselves, but still have thirteen babies and suck the welfare system dry. I mean those who can't afford proper food and clothing for their children, but still manage to acquire a mouth-full of gold teeth.

I'm talking about ghetto slang, thick gold chains, handguns in backpacks and spinning hubcaps. I'm talking about niggers.

I have always been criticized for my attitude toward the black culture. It probably has a lot to do with my skin color. If I was fair-skinned with sandy-colored hair and freckles, I would be just another racist not even worth mentioning. But I am what they call an "Uncle Tom." My skin is as dark as the tires on your car, but I am no nigger.

The woman who gave birth to me was a nigger, and so was the man who impregnated her. Luckily for me, I did not spend more than a few minutes with those people before I was signed over as just another orphan in the system. And then I was adopted by two of the most honest and caring people in the world.

My parents are church-going, Merle Haggard-loving, blue-collared Republicans who brought me up just as they would have any daughter who shared their pale complexion. I love my parents with all of my heart.

I have never fit in with the black community.

My church and neighborhood are both predominantly white. My old high school was mostly white and Hispanic. The small black student population always stuck together, usually only shunning those blacks who were deemed socially awkward, like myself. I don't swear excessively, smoke marijuana in the parking lot or have sex in the restrooms, so I was not accepted by them. I never complained.

Needless to say, I never had a boyfriend in high school. The white guys were afraid I'd be just another hood rat with a dirty mouth and reputation. The black guys talked to me just long enough to figure out that I wasn't just an easy lay like the rest of their girlfriends. That's how it was in college, as well. Rare was the occasion someone spoke to me unless it involved something we were working on in class. And that is how I came to meet Dylan.

He and I shared some college classes during our freshman year, but as we were both somewhat shy, we never spoke to each other. Then one day in our Music Appreciation class, there was a discussion about how American rock 'n roll music had been separated into categories that defined the listener of any band or performer who fell into each respective category.

It was said that those who listened to the Beach Boys or Jan and Dean had to be part of the California surf culture. Fans of the Jefferson Airplane and Strawberry Alarm Clock were said to be obvious druggies caught up in the acid wave. Fans of the Allman Brothers Band and Lynyrd Skynyrd were Southern rednecks, and therefore supporters of slavery and racism. Fans of Pete Seeger and Joan Baez, however, were the intelligent ones who opposed racism and the government's illegal war in Vietnam.

Nobody seemed to have a problem with the rationale of the instructor or the other students except for me and Dylan. Although we were ridiculed for supposedly knowing nothing about how music plays a role in society, we were instantly drawn to each other. I thought he was cute and funny, and I am sure he was just intrigued by how a young, black girl could even know who Pete Seeger and the Allman Brothers were. He approached me after class a few days later and asked if I wanted to go to the record store and help him pick out some new music to buy. I thought he was joking, but I agreed to go with him. Well, that night was followed with another date that included a movie. And then there was a dinner date and then he was invited by my parents to come over for supper. He and my parents bonded quickly, and he immediately got their approval to continue taking me out.

Getting approval from Dylan's father, however, seemed next to impossible. Dylan swears that his dad isn't a racist, but I know he is when it comes to the subject of who his son is dating. And I know that I might not look like what Mr. Boudreau had pictured as the perfect woman for his son, but it could all be much, much worse. I mean, at least Dylan isn't gay.

As time went on and Dylan and I grew closer, we realized that both of us wanted to become schoolteachers. It may have been fate or just coincidence, but our not-so-normal childhoods made us both eager to pursue careers that would enable us to help children grow during their formative years.

Getting through college was no big deal for me. I am smart and a hard worker, so the schoolwork was always easy for me. Plus, my parents could afford to pay the tuition, so that was one less thing for me to worry about.

Dylan, however, didn't have it so easy. Although he is extremely intelligent, he doesn't come from what most people consider to be a stable family, let alone a wealthy one. His mother has never been in the picture, and his father's constant state of intoxication has always made the picture a little blurry. The only way Dylan could afford to pay for school alone was to work full-time while attending a community college, and it looked as though it was going to take several years to complete his degree. Dylan had decided early on that the best opportunity for his future was to pursue the option his father was robbed of so many years earlier.

Though we started college at the same time, when I had only one year left before completion,

Dylan still had almost three. It would have been much quicker if he had gone into the Air Force right after high school. They would have helped him through college, and after four years, he would have gotten out of the service with a college degree and military experience. But living the dream his father wasn't able to live would have broken Mr. Boudreau's heart. It would have been bittersweet for him, I'm sure. To see Dylan strive for excellence and actually achieve it would have probably been the proudest moment in his father's life, but seeing his own son living with the honor while he himself has been reduced to a handicapped alcoholic would have been too much for his tired heart to handle.

And so to spare his father's feelings, Dylan pushed on through the community college and never acted on his Air Force dreams.

I always wondered if avoiding hurting Mr. Boudreau's feelings was actually hurting Dylan's chances of success. The one time I brought it up with him, he recited a piece of poetry he found on a scrap of paper in his closet, which was still full of his father's old things. The poem was short and simple, and it urged the reader to push forward in the face of hardship. Though Dylan received it indirectly, he considered the message of the poem to be the only piece of advice his father ever gave him, and so he thought it was important to honor it and not take the easy way through life. This meant he would work harder than most people do, but at least he would have a clear conscience to go with his American Dream, whenever he would finally began to live it.

Hard workers as we were, Dylan and I made plans and stuck to them. A few months before I graduated from college, Dylan proposed to me. I accepted, of course, and we decided the big day would be two weeks after graduation. We also decided that before I actively started searching for a teaching position, we would go ahead and start our family while we were both still young. With any hope, we figured, I would become pregnant soon after we got married, and we would be well on our way to a happy life together.

Dylan was driven, always working for our future, and never forgetting how hard we would all have to work to be happy. With the wedding day in the near future, we were both praying and hoping that I would be able to become pregnant when the time was right. I was close to finishing college, and Dylan's education was moving along with an increased momentum. We were so close to the perfect life. It was almost within our grasp.

And then Dylan's mother showed up.

CHAPTER EIGHT:
THE RETURN OF A MOTHER

I bet my son fucks all the time. I don't know if that sort of thing is genetical or not, but if that's something passed down to a child, he probably fucks a lot. I sure know I did my share of screwing when I was younger, but most of it was done for business purposes, so that probably doesn't count. And I know his daddy liked to fuck, and so did my daddy. They both liked to fuck *me*, at least.

The only reason I say that about my boy is because he's such a handsome man, and I'm sure he has the ladies lined up around the corner, all of them just waiting for a chance to get with him.

He sure is a fine-looking young man, if I do say so myself. I sure know how to make a good-looking baby.

My son was taller than his daddy. I mean, even if his daddy had legs, my son would still be taller. Probably.

I was actually hoping to see both of them that night in the Mexican restaurant, but as my son came up to the table, I saw that he didn't have his daddy rolling along beside him.

"Hey, mom," he said as he sat down. "Dad couldn't make it. He already had some plans that he couldn't get out of tonight."

"Yeah, that's too bad. I'm sure he's got a lot to tell me." I knew Arthur wouldn't show up. I know he still has bad feelings about me. "So, what do they call you these days? Is it Artie, or Art?"

"No, actually it's Dylan," he said. "It's just a nickname, I guess, but that's what everyone always calls me."

"What did you take as a middle name?" I asked, still curious after all these years to find out what Arthur's middle name was.

"Still don't have one, but it wasn't a big deal when I was born, so it can't really matter now."

"Yeah," I said, not knowing if that was a nice way of telling me that I fucked up or not. "I'm sorry about that, but I just figured your daddy was gonna be there to help fill in the blanks, but he wasn't able to make it in that night, neither."

"Yeah, but he's been there for me every day since."

I was beginning to feel the burn from his eyes on my forehead. So I quit fighting while I still had someone there to fight with. We moved on to more pleasant topics, like what happened to me since I left him with his daddy all those years ago. I tried to leave out the parts that were unbecoming of a fine mother, like all the drugs and fucking and such, but I know I accidentally slipped some of it in when I was talking too fast to let my thoughts catch up.

After I left my baby with that monster who is his father, I had no reason to live anymore — or no reason to stay in San Antonio, at least. So I went back to El Paso. After trying the waitress thing for a while, I remembered why I always hated it so much. So I went back to doing what I did best, which was anything a guy would pay me to do. At least it earned me enough money to get by, but if the truth must be known, I've never really enjoyed being a prostitute.

Anyways, this one dude I was fucking this one time said he thought I had what it takes to be a movie star. As it turns out, he just thought I could take it like a champ in any position and in any hole, so he was merely saying that I could make it as a pornographic video actress. Either way he meant it, I took it as a compliment.

I ran the idea through my head for a long, long

time. And then the next day I skipped out on the rent and got on a bus and started my trip to Los Angeles. I was gonna try out for every movie audition I could, except for porn movies. I did have standards, after all. I mean, I'd take it in the ass by two guys at once, but I'd never so much as lick a nut if it was gonna be caught on video tape. I had a son somewhere out there in the world and I couldn't imagine the embarrassment he would feel if he ever realized he was jerking off to a porno video his mama starred in.

As it turned out, in order to be in a movie in California, you have to be part of that big union thing, which costed something like fifteen hundred bucks a year. Only someone who was already making movies could afford to pay that kind of money to join their club, so I had to go back to hooking just to pay the bills and such. And then I was introduced to this guy, James, who was a buddy of this guy I fucked on a regular basis, and James was into drugs. He got me to sell the cocaine to some of the guys I was fucking, and James would pay me a lot of cash. We started running a deal where I'd give the dude whatever service he asked for and I wouldn't even charge him for it just so long as he bought some of the coke at the prices that James charged. Then James would pay me for the fuck and give me a little bit extra.

A couple of times, these big black guys would beat the shit out of me, rape me and then run off with the cocaine. Then James would beat me even more for letting these guys have the shit without paying. James was a real asshole sometimes.

But, yeah, that's how I got arrested that last time down there. I was all bloodied in a parking lot after this big nigger and James both kicked the shit out of me, and someone called for an ambulance. When the cops came to the hospital to ask questions and such, they found some coke in my purse that James and the big nigger both missed. I was charged with possession and I spent almost a month in jail. When I got out, I hopped on the first bus back to El Paso.

Once back home, I went back to being a waitress and put all that hooking shit behind me. I met this guy at the diner I worked at who owned his own plumbing company. Me and Larry — that's the plumber guy — we got married after we'd been dating for like four months.

We had the perfect life together. Larry had his own company truck and shirts with his name on them and everything. And we lived in the house that Larry's daddy owned for thirty years and it had a lawn and a fence and everything. We were happy for close to eight years, and all we needed to be complete was a baby of our own. Larry had two grown kids from his dead ex-wife, and since my baby boy was stolen away from me, all me and Larry needed was a baby to share between us. We tried and tried for years to get me knocked up, but it was taking forever for God to bless us in that way.

And then Larry started fucking this seventeen-year-old girl who answered the phones at his plumbing company and she got herself pregnant by my husband. So Larry threw me out on my ass and moved this girl in to sleep on my side of the bed. That stupid little slut.

So, once again, I was out on my own. And since the house and the plumbing company and all that stuff technically belonged to Larry's daddy, I couldn't even get half of it in the divorce. I got shit.

By this time I was just too old to make a decent wage hooking, and since I really didn't like doing it in the first place, I decided to go back to doing the second thing that I was always pretty good at doing, which was waitressing. And so I got me a new boyfriend really quickly and moved in with him to save on the rent, and when I knew things were going pretty rocky with us, I simply went out and got a different boyfriend. The last thing I wanted was to be outdoors.

But moving around from guy to guy like that got pretty old pretty fast, so about five years after Larry divorced me, I moved on out to San Antonio again. I found that same truck stop where I worked before I met Arthur, but they changed the name of it some years ago. Well, they hired me on that same day I rolled into town. And then I went just around the corner and found that same little hotel I lived at when I worked at the truck stop before. It still has the same name, but even though it's twenty years older now, it's a lot cleaner than it was back then. I got a room there.

After almost three months, I decided to go ahead and look for my baby boy, only he was a grown man by this time. I didn't even know where to start. I eventually found Arthur's name in a phone book, though I wasn't sure if it was for my boy or for his daddy. It didn't specify, and there was also no number listed. But it did have an address. And that's when I decided that I should get over there to patch up whatever problems still existed between me and Arthur, or me and my baby, whichever one it was living there at that address.

"Wow," Dylan said after I brought him up to speed on my life so far. "I never knew how hard of a life you had. I never knew how hard you've worked to get here."

"Yeah, all I've ever done is work hard," I replied. I wanted him to know that he's always been in my thoughts, and that I have always hoped that we would be like a mother and son again.

"Well, you're here now, and you found me. Where does it go from here?" he asked.

"I really don't know, honestly," I said. "I never thought I'd really be back in this city again, let alone sitting down with my son."

"Yeah, it's pretty unreal," he agreed. "One day soon, maybe you can meet my girlfriend. She's really a nice girl, and I'm sure she'd like to meet you, too. And maybe you and dad can actually have a conversation. I'm sure enough time has passed that you two can put everything behind you and maybe be friendly again. You know, like adults?"

"Oh, yeah, sure," I said reassuringly. "I just wanna get to know you better and not fight about the past with your father. That's all."

"If you spend too much time looking into the rear-view mirror, you'll crash into whatever is in front of you," Dylan said, poetically enough. "I heard that somewhere."

"It's very true," I said. "And it also reminds me of something I've been meaning to ask you about."

CHAPTER NINE:
THE BURDEN OF A SON

My mother really is a dirty whore.

Sometimes you really need to mess your entire life up to realize how messed up everyone else in your life really is.

I was taken advantage of by my own mother, and I should've seen it coming. That's what she's done her whole life, to everyone she has ever known. And I let her do it to me. Now I know why my father always said he wished he had burned her alive all those years ago.

She really does bring out the worst in people.

I met her for dinner one night, and she told me her life story, and what a sob story it was.

Although trashy at most times, she did have a quality to her that demands pity. And I gave it to her.

She couldn't stop talking about how straight and narrow her life would be from here on out, how all the bad things she'd ever done in her life were now all things of the past, simple memories that were not even worth remembering.

She had a roof over her head and a stable job to pay the rent. All she lacked was a mode of transportation. Walking to work in the rain, it seemed, wasn't allowing her to keep up her professional appearance at the diner and she was afraid she'd be fired soon if either the rain wouldn't let up or she couldn't buy a car soon. I asked her why she just didn't ride the bus, but she said that the nearest bus stop to her home was actually right in front of her job.

Her big doe eyes really sealed the deal, and I reluctantly agreed to loan her the money she needed to buy a cheap automobile. I later found out that I was agreeing to give up my entire life and everything I ever knew and loved, just so my mother could get another free ride.

I really didn't have the money to loan to her. All the money I had was what Alexis and I had saved up so we could buy wedding rings. It was a lot of money. We really didn't need the most expensive rings, but that wasn't the point. It was our money, and I handed it over to someone I really didn't know. She was supposed to pay me back within the next month and a half. Needless to say, she didn't pay me back.

Alexis was angry from the moment I told her. She's always been smarter than me, I guess, so she would've been able to identify the problem before it ever started. But I'm not as smart as her. That must be the reason I decided to lie to Alexis about it in the first place and just hope that my mother paid me back before Alexis found out the money was missing from our bank account.

After two weeks and not a single penny back from my mother, I grew quite scared of what Alexis would say if she found out. And then she found out. And she was very angry about it.

"What were you thinking?" she shouted. "That was the money for our wedding!"

"No, your dad is paying for the wedding," I countered. "That money was for our rings, which we don't technically need in order to be married."

"Yes!" she screamed. "You do need rings to get married! It's all part of the deal. It's a ceremony that requires rings and now we don't have money to buy our rings!"

"We're going to get the money back long before we need to buy the rings," I explained. "And even if the worse happened and we weren't able to get the rings we wanted before the wedding, we could buy cheaper rings to use in the ceremony and then replace them with the better ones after we actually got married."

According to her, that was the dumbest idea

she had ever heard of. She didn't want to use "fake" wedding rings in the ceremony. The rings were symbolic of our love and of our holy union in marriage, and if we simply threw away our wedding rings and replaced them with shinier imposters, what would keep us from simply throwing away our vows and replacing them with something else later on down the road?

I could sort of see her point, but damn....

Without the rings, we couldn't get married, Alexis said. And we both agreed that asking her parents to buy them for us was out of the question.

A whole month went by and my mother said she was still working on getting the money together. I explained to her that we really needed the money and that if she could give us anything at all, it would be helpful. My mother said she had to buy a new transmission almost as soon as she bought the car and that she didn't have anything left of her savings after that.

Alexis said that we were left with no other option but to postpone the wedding a few months. We told everyone that it was so we could plan it more thoroughly. It was all just a weak lie, but it bought us some time.

After two months of hounding my mother with unreturned phone messages, her phone was disconnected. I went to see her at the hotel she said she was staying at, but she had left without paying the rent for the last two weeks.

That didn't sit too well with Alexis. At that point, it wasn't even about the money anymore, but about the fact that someone had ripped us off, that the "someone" was my own mother, and that I was stupid enough to let it happen.

The arguments between us got pretty bad by that time. And Alexis, during one of our "make-up, break-up" sessions, had accidentally gotten pregnant. It was just a really bad time.

"I told you that bitch was no good," my father said the day I moved my stuff back into his apartment. "Her kind is always doing something like that."

"Who are you talking about this time?" I asked. "Are you talking about Alexis or my mother?"

"Both of them, actually," he said with just a hint of humor. "Them negro bitches are always taking a man's money and then sending him packing. But I was really talking about your mother. I told you that bitch just wanted something from you. I told you that you just couldn't trust her. Ain't you been listening for twenty years?"

"Yeah, well you trusted her once," I reminded him.

"Yeah, and you should've learned from my mistake," he demanded.

And he was right. I have been told my whole life that if there was one person in the whole world who simply couldn't be trusted, it was my own mother. And I trusted her with the one thing that would turn even the most trustworthy person into a rat, which was money. I acted as carelessly as a person who leaves his expensive sports car running in the parking lot while he goes inside for a latte, as recklessly as a man who walks his dog, unleashed, along a busy freeway, or as blindly as those parents who continually allowed their children to spend the night at Michael Jackson's house.

The bottom line is that I should have known the consequences of my actions, but I failed to heed the warnings. I have nobody to blame for any of this but myself.

Alexis was the first to get on my case about it, telling me how stupid I was. My father was the second person, immediately after my fiancé, telling me he told me so. And it was my father who gave me a place to stay after Alexis threw me out of our apartment and out of her life. Personally, I think she overacted.

She said that I had thrown our entire wedding away, thus throwing away any happiness we could possibly have in our future. I didn't consider having to postpone our wedding as "throwing it away," but I'm a guy. What do I know?

Her parents wouldn't have been overly happy with the thought of their daughter possibly having a child born out of wedlock, so that made things worse. As conservatively as she had been raised, I never thought she'd go so far as to have an abortion, but that is exactly what she did. She walked into one of those clinics and paid a so-called doctor to remove our baby and kill it there in his office.

Up until that point, I actually thought that this was all just a minor set-back with me and Alexis. But apparently, it had been over for her that day I decided to loan my own mother a few thousand dollars. Who knew that an act of kindness would end up ruining my life?

She never even told me that she'd had the abortion. I had to find out through mutual friends. It was also the way I found out she had moved on up to Austin after graduation and become immediately involved with the kind of guy she has always loathed — a common ghetto thug.

He apparently has a fine job washing cars over at some import auto dealership. She is a stay-at-home mom now, not putting her education or her teaching credentials to any sort of use.

It was a little over a year and a half later, right about the time I heard she had her second child, that I decided to finally join the Air Force. At that point in time, it was no longer my dream life, nor that of my father's, but it seemed that life had dealt me a horrible hand, and I figured that it was far worse to simply fold than to ask the dealer for another card.

Because of the fact that I had a college degree by that time, I was put through officer candidate school and commissioned as a second lieutenant. But instead of the life of a fighter pilot, which is what I thought I was ordering, I was instead served the life of an administrations officer and sent to Colorado Springs to warm some chair behind some computer in some cubicle in some office.

Needless to say, I never made any attempt to contact Alexis again, and I just always assumed she was content with her fate.

I continued to search for my mother after she disappeared. I initially wanted to explain to her how she had destroyed the life of her only child, but I figured she would never be able to understand something like that. Then I decided to simply go after her for the money that she owed me. But she vanished into thin air, back to the arms of another pathetic loser of a man who would carry her load until she tired of him. Or maybe it was back to some desolate truck stop diner somewhere on the outskirts of some dirty Texas town. But most likely, I reckoned, is that she is standing, this very moment in time, on the corner of some sleazy street, earning a dollar the only way she has ever been prosperous.

My father, however, is someone I had always thought would be there for me. But while I was going through my Air Force training, he seemed to have simply vanished, too. His not having a telephone meant that I could only communicate with him through mailed letters, and he failed to ever write me back. I guess maybe he felt as though I had abandoned him by leaving after he had allowed me to move back in and stay there for almost two years. Whatever the case, by the time I got to Colorado Springs, the letters were marked "Return to Sender." I never heard from him again.

It was actually Father Silva who eventually contacted me. I had failed to let him know that I was leaving town to join the military, and it was he who eventually tracked me down, because my father wasn't able to do so himself.

CHAPTER TEN:
THE DESTINY OF A GIRL

White folks are some fucked-up motherfuckers. There are some exceptions to that statement, but they are few. My adoptive parents, for instance, are perfect examples of the rare exception. My former fiancé, however, is not. And neither is any member of his family. They're the most fucked-up motherfuckers I've ever seen.

I was brainwashed by the white culture. Aside from my ebony skin, I was basically white. Hell, I still ain't got my natural rhythm back. I still can't dance.

I don't blame my adoptive parents for raising me like that. They just did what they thought was right at the time. Now they know that it wasn't right, but now it's too late. The damage is already done. And though I don't hold them personally responsible for robbing me of my culture, I no longer speak to them. I know they realize deep down in their hearts that it's for the best.

Being part of the white culture, I grew up with the backwards belief that you're always supposed to look out for number one. That belief is the reason why you'll never see any white gangs running around. You see political parties made up of old white men, but each party member is only there for his own personal gain. A presidential debate is the closest any white man has gotten to a gang war. The Ku Klux Klan is sometimes called a gang, but it is actually just a political party that is more visibly violent than the Democrats and Republicans.

While black street gangs have a bad reputation based on the violence their images now represent, the overall goal of the gangs is very noble. What the white law enforcement officials label as "gangs" are nothing more than groups of like-minded individuals from the same social and economic backgrounds who simply want to better the environment in which they live, work and raise their children. But because the white society is so afraid of a "negro uprising," they outlaw groups of African Americans from peacefully gathering without a permit, they refuse to issue them permits, and then they throw them in jail for violating the RICO Act, which was specifically designed by the federal government to fill the prisons with black men.

Those within the black society are left with no choice but to fight to feed their families. That is why there is so much perceived territorial disputes that result in so-called gang violence. When these people are persecuted and they aren't even allowed to work honestly for their income, they sometimes must resort to drug dealing and even common thievery just to get by.

All of this is a direct result of the racism and selfishness naturally instilled in each and every white person, especially Americans.

White people could never truly understand what it really means to be part of a family. Sure, they marry their high school sweetheart and reproduce, but their spouse and offspring become nothing more than extensions of themselves. Everything they do is for the benefit of only them.

Black people, on the other hand, want only to better their culture and society and every individual black person knows that they are each an important part of the bigger picture. White people are too individualistic to ever understand this concept.

I was deeply rooted within the white culture, so I wasn't able to see it for myself at the time. I was even engaged to be married to one of them, and it was our breakup that eventually allowed me to see the truth.

Dylan gave all of our life's savings to his mother, who mysteriously showed up twenty years after she abandoned him. If my birth mother was to suddenly show up out of the blue, I wouldn't even give her the time of day, let alone all of my money. But that is exactly what Dylan did. He wasn't thinking about anybody but himself and how much he wanted a mother so badly that he felt he had to basically buy one off the street.

A guy who I knew from school always questioned why I was with a white guy. Tyrell said I was too dark to be with someone so pale. At first, he seemed to be almost flirting with me, but then he came across later as just downright mean. He said I was disrespecting my ancestors and myself by dating a white guy. And though he hurt my feelings on several occasions, Tyrell became almost a friend to me. He was certainly someone I could talk to, at least.

Having nobody else, I reluctantly confided in Tyrell when Dylan and I were having our troubles. I really just wanted a male's point of view of the situation, and instead received the "black" point of view. He told me to leave Dylan, but I refused because I still thought I loved him then.

Tyrell was eventually able to convince me to go out with him and some friends after school for some dinner. I had always turned down his invitations before because I really didn't feel comfortable with the idea of going out with a bunch of people I didn't know. Finally, the day Dylan moved all his stuff out of our apartment, the idea seemed less uncomfortable than the thought of going back to my apartment alone.

We met up with some of Tyrell's friends at a barbecue chicken restaurant because Tyrell said that I needed to get back to my roots. He even ordered me a grape soda. It was supposed help make me feel black, he said.

After dinner, we all went back to Tyrell's house, which he shared with his girlfriend and his brother, Jerome. They had the music turned up really loud and somebody was playing the role of bartender. There were probably a couple dozen people there, and they were all drinking and insisting that I also drink. I finally gave in, but because I was pregnant, I asked the guy mixing the drinks to make all of my beverages nonalcoholic. I guess he forgot that very important request, because about an hour into the party, it felt like the room was spinning completely around me. Not too long after that, because the alcohol had lowered my inhibitions and judgment, they were able to convince me to smoke a marijuana cigarette with them.

One thing led to another, and not too long after that, I found myself involved in sexual intercourse with Tyrell, Jerome and some other guy. When they were all finished, one of their friends who had been watching and possibly taking pictures, made me go down on him.

Later on that night, after the music died down and many of the people there had left, there was some discussion as to who would be responsible for getting me out of their house. I was still pretty wasted, but I do recall Tyrell reminding them all that he already had a girlfriend and that I should go to his brother. I passed out after that and awoke on the floor next to some people I did not remember meeting the night before.

In the early afternoon, Jerome gave me a ride back to my apartment, and being the gentleman that he is, he walked me all the way up to my door. Still not entirely experienced with proper dating rituals, I felt obligated to invite Jerome inside.

He accepted, and he waited on the couch while I showered and changed into some clean clothes.

We talked for a few hours about our lives and we just got to know each other. I told him of my school and my parents and of Dylan. Jerome told me of his plans in life, which included dropping out of high school his senior year of high school so he could work on his music career, which he said was going to make him rich and famous one day. He was also a champion basketball player, being virtually unbeatable in his old neighborhood. He could have gotten a basketball scholarship to any university of his choice, but he declined because he knew he was good enough to skip a four-year college and go straight into the professional draft. But a racist cop arrested him for supposedly driving without insurance on a suspended license in a car that was reported stolen, even though his neighbor told him that he could drive it. He avoided prison time by pleading guilty to the made-up charges and was placed on house arrest for a while. Needless to say, that took away any chances he had of going into the professional basketball draft.

When I mentioned to Jerome that I was pregnant with Dylan's baby, he asked why I didn't just get an abortion since I was no longer with Dylan. I explained to him that our separation was just temporary and that we'd be getting back together after our cooling-off period. But Jerome explained to me how white men are. He opened my eyes to the fact that Dylan was never coming back to me and that he probably already had another girlfriend. That girl was definitely Caucasian. White people are naturally racist, whether they know it or not. They're just more comfortable with other pale-faced, selfish individuals.

That being the case, I had to sit down with Jerome and really think long and hard about whether or not I wanted to go along with the pregnancy. I looked at the situation from every possible angle. We stayed up so late talking that Jerome ended up staying the night, and the next morning he drove me to the clinic and I had my mistake surgically removed.

It was a good two months before I was pregnant again, but this time it was with a good and strong purebred African baby boy. He was conceived at another one of those house parties and Jerome was most likely the father.

Almost a year later, we had a little girl, followed by another little boy the year after that. Those two were definitely Jerome's babies.

Eventually, we moved to Austin and Jerome got a full-time job detailing luxury automobiles. We got our own apartment, got married and I became a stay-at-home mother.

And for the first time I could remember, my life was great.

CONCLUSION:
THE RESIGNATION OF A PRIEST

God can go fuck Himself. I mean He could if He even exists in the first place, which is a concept that I very much doubt now. If there is such a Supreme Being, the very one that I have based my entire life on, then I am now afraid that He is not the all-loving deity we have all been raised to worship and praise.

I was raised to believe that all things, for which we initially perceive to be good or ill, are of God's will. Then, after I became a man of the cloth, it was my job to educate others on this belief. No matter what happens in life, everything is for the best in the end of it all, because it all happens just as the Lord plans.

If that's the case, fuck the Lord.

It was the night after her funeral that I was awakened in the middle of the night by what my nightmare had me to believe was the fires of Hell, burning right outside of my bedroom window. It was a very fitting end of a day that I really wished had not involved me at all.

The service was quick. Nobody showed up except me and her, and a few older women who always attend the funerals held at our church. They didn't know the deceased, and neither did I, for that matter. All I knew of her was from stories Arthur told me of her hard life, and I also knew of how she passed on.

She died in her sleep, and I'd like to think that is was a peaceful journey from this life to the next, but I know that the moments leading to her body's eternal slumber were not calm ones.

On the nightstand next to the hotel room bed in which she died was a torn envelope with a letter stuffed back inside. The letter was to her son, Dylan, and it explained her reasons for ignoring him as of late. She was embarrassed for having to take his money, and even more so, she was embarrassed by the friction she had caused between him and his intended wife. But, as she wrote in the letter, she had finally saved up enough money to pay him back, along with a little extra as a wedding present.

When the police finally found her body, however, there was no money in the envelope. She was found with a belt cinched tightly around her left arm, and the syringe was still dangling from the vein. Other than the one caused by that needle, there were no other recent track marks on her body. As it appeared, she had kept her word about staying clean in hopes of repairing her shattered life, and her practically non-existent relationship with her son.

The police believe she was murdered for the cash she kept in her hotel room. The room showed signs of a struggle and the amount of heroine she still had in her system was enough to kill even the most hardened addict three times over. There were no signs of a forced entry into her room, so her killer is believed to be someone she knew. The police had no suspects and the case went cold just as quickly as it had been opened. And with no way to reach any family members, her body was turned over to the county for burial.

I asked for custody of her body so that she could be given a proper Christian burial, and the county officials were more than happy to be rid of her. The church paid for her casket and donated a plot in our small cemetery.

I went to Arthur's apartment to let him know of Ms. Carroll's death, but he did not answer the door. I knew he was at home, because it was well before noon. And so I pounded hard on his door to wake him, and eventually I heard some movement from behind his door.

"Open up, Arthur," I bellowed from where his welcome mat would be, had he laid one out to make anybody feel welcome. "It's me. I've got to talk to you about something."

He never answered back, but I knew he was listening.

"It's about Dylan's mother. Arthur, she'd dead. Please let me in."

This lasted for a good five minutes, and I eventually gave up any notion that he would actually open the door.

"Her funeral will be tomorrow, Arthur, at eleven o'clock. I really hope you'll be there."

He wasn't there. And neither was Dylan. I had no idea where the boy was, and I knew Arthur had lost touch with him some time ago.

Later on that night, I was awakened from a nightmare. I don't remember exactly what it was about, but I awoke in a cold sweat, and I was scared of something. My bedroom window was glowing bright, and I knew that it was a fire. Almost afraid to see what was burning, I hesitated to draw the curtains.

At the edge of the walkway up to the church, down where it meets the sidewalk, one of the two huge, green bushes was in flames. The sight of it snapped me out of whatever daze I had been in and I hurried to throw on my bathrobe and rush out the door.

The thought to grab the fire extinguisher on my way out somehow never entered into my mind, and I found myself racing toward the burning shrubbery empty-handed and unable to put out the flames. But still I raced toward it, somehow believing it would be better to get to the fire than to go back for the extinguisher.

As I approached the bush, I suddenly felt helpless about being able to do something to put out the flames. The fire, being at the edge of the lawn near the sidewalk, was of no immediate threat to anything other than the other bush. Looking back on it, I must have looked pretty silly to the neighbors as I scrambled and panicked at the small shrub set ablaze, but it just seemed more threatening at the time.

Just as I began to calm myself down, my eyes focused on the center of the small fire, where the flames glowed the deepest red against the green stems, branches and leaves. I couldn't move my eyes from that spot. I was paralyzed in that standing position, concentrating deeply against my will on the center of the fire. It was if it had hypnotized me and wouldn't let me go. It was speaking to me, but I couldn't hear any sounds. My peripheral vision filled with the flashing red tips of the flame as it grew around me, completely surrounding me and still not letting me move.

I was thrust onto the ground behind me, as if I had been pulled from the back, and then the water completely drenched the bush and put out the fire. The fireman who pulled me back away from the bush informed me that a neighbor had called the fire department because it appeared I wasn't able to control the fire and she feared it might burn down the church. I couldn't bring myself to explain to him that I hadn't even tried to contain it.

"That's a durable bush you've got there," joked another fireman after he was sure he had completely put out the flames.

The bush looked as though there was never any fire at all. The surrounding area was soaked, but the bush itself was unburned.

The fireman in charge said the fire was probably caused by some delinquent kids out past their curfew with a cigarette lighter and nothing better to do. Then he advised me to fill out a report with the police department the first thing in the morning. Instead, as soon as the big, red fire engine rolled away, I went to the tool shed around the back side of the church, brought out a shovel and dug up the flammable shrubbery. And just to keep things symmetrical, I dug out its companion. I threw them both into the dumpster and flattened out the dirt where the bushes formerly stood.

The next night I received a call from the county coroner's office, which informed me that I had another body to sign out from them.

"I think I may have given you the wrong

impression the other day," I informed the man on the other end of the line. "This one church really can't afford to pay funeral and burial costs for each and every homeless soul who passes away within the county."

"But this one's got your name on it," he said. "The note says that this one belongs to you. Do you know an Arthur Boudreau?"

The bloody note in Arthur's wallet simply stated, "Call Father Silva. He'll know what to do." It had my phone number scribbled next to my name, and the investigators thought it looked like a personal reminder Arthur had written to himself. I explained to them that Arthur never used the telephone and that it was obviously instructions for whoever was in charge of disposing of his body. Arthur always thought that I was the one with the answers, but at that point, all I had was questions.

Tired, both physically and mentally, I made the arrangements for Arthur's body to be delivered to the mortuary, and then for one last ride to the church, where he'd be buried near the mother of his only son. I went down to an Air Force recruiting office to seek their help in finding Dylan. They couldn't help me, but suggested that I ask the Red Cross for assistance. They placed a call to Dylan's command and passed the information regarding both of his parents' deaths on to them. I never heard anything back from Dylan.

I held a funeral for Arthur similar to that of Ms. Carroll, and the attendance was the same. The eulogy was similar, as well. I not only lacked the time to write anything new, but I also lacked any inspiration to do so. I could find nothing positive to say about this man who chose to ignore anything positive in his life. He chose to dwell in the negative until he lost everyone and everything that meant anything to him. Life to him was a series of bad events. It was as if he was addicted to feeling bad, until he couldn't even find any pleasure in even *that* anymore and he rolled his wheelchair onto the freeway and into the path of a semi truck.

The truck driver said Arthur made no attempt to exit the roadway, and instead rolled his chair toward the speeding truck. By the time his truck's headlights lit up the area around Arthur, there was not enough time to stop the truck.

It was determined on the official police report to have been an accident, caused when the poor, intoxicated man in the wheelchair made the bad decision to attempt to cross the interstate and chance his luck with the traffic.

But anybody who ever met Arthur would have known that he wasn't betting against the traffic, but rather counting on it to take him away.

I don't know what made me do it, but two nights after he was laid to rest, I decided to retrace Arthur's final moments. I put on my blue jeans, my jacket and my sneakers and walked to his apartment. That was to be my starting point, where Arthur no doubt started his final journey.

His apartment was empty now, as I had spent the entire day before clearing out all of his belongings. I threw away most of it and boxed up the things I hoped to eventually give to Dylan if I ever saw him again.

Among Arthur's possessions was a box of cash. Apparently, Arthur no longer had faith in any banks, so for the past several years, he had deposited all of his cash into that brown box in his closet. I hoped the money would now be able to help Dylan on his path to success in the absence of his loved ones.

I stepped inside the apartment, looked around one last time, and left, closing the door slowly behind me. I was expecting the clicking sound made as the door came to a stop to serve as some form of closure for me, as if it would lock Arthur out of my mind and I could simply move on in a positive direction. But that wasn't the case, so I started my walk.

I always used the stairs every other time I went to and from his front door, even a day earlier while carrying several heavy boxes down. But Arthur did not take the stairs on his final outing, nor had he ever taken those stairs once in the decades he had lived in the apartment. So I stepped into the thick metal box and rode the elevator down to the ground floor below.

I continued along the sidewalk, out the gates of the apartment complex, and along the street. I strolled slowly past the little corner liquor store Arthur no doubt bought his drink from. There were men inside doing just that, and they caught my stare as I passed by them, and they glared back at me in disgust of my perceived criticism. I wondered if they would have even looked me in the eyes had I been wearing my white collar.

I saw a prostitute who puckered her lips as I passed, and I imagined Ms. Carroll standing in her place many years ago. This young girl stands to endure the same fate Dylan's mother faced. I could try to help this young girl, but then what? As soon as she moves, another young hooker will stand in her place. The cycle will continue, time and time again, and it will always end the same. It's a losing battle. That girl's a lost cause.

By the time I reached the hotel where Ms. Carroll died, it was starting to rain. It was just a light sprinkle at that point, but knowing San Antonio weather, that meant nothing. It was either going to continue sprinkling, misting just enough moisture to dampen my jacket, or it was going to start a downpour that would flood the streets and threaten me with a soggy demise along the poorly lit streets on that side of town. Or, if I was absolutely lucky enough, the rain would cease all together in just a minute or two, and the rest of my pilgrimage would be a dry and comfortable one. I was a long way from my destination, but also a long way from home, so I wagered my dry socks and kept on walking.

I lost my own bet, and the dryness of my socks and shoes and everything I had on me was the cost. As I made it about halfway through an unlit stretch of sidewalk along a vacant lot that I was sure was just recently a row of low-income housing, the Lord really tested my determination to finish my march. The rain came down in bucket loads and I actually began to wonder what it felt like to die by drowning.

I picked up my pace quite a bit and ran to a neon-lit building within an expansive parking lot of semi trucks and busses. I decided to take a seat inside the truck stop until the rain let up. A hot cup of coffee and a slice of pie might be comforting, I thought.

"What can I get you?" the waitress asked, chomping on her gum and whipping out her notepad. She looked as though she had worked there her whole life, for about as long as the truck stop had been there, I imagined.

"How about a towel?" I asked. Maybe I was joking; I don't really know. I think she thought I was, at least.

"I'd get you one, you know, but Hector would get pissed at me again," she said back with a smile. "He washes the dishes in the back, and he's always concerned about the health code violations and stuff. Says you can't dry a plate with a towel after you done used it to dry off a man's head."

"Hector sounds like a really smart guy."

"Nah, he barely speaks any English. And I don't think he's even supposed to be here, you know." She chomped on her gum a few more times. "But other than a towel, is there anything else I can get for you?"

I ordered my lemon pie and coffee, and the waitress told me that there was probably enough paper towels left in the men's room to dry my hair. I told her I'd be right back, and I made my way to the back of the diner, in the direction she had pointed.

I wasn't the only drenched man at the truck stop that night, it seemed. I had to practically wade my way through the discarded paper towels as soon as I entered the restroom, and I squeezed past about half a dozen men all doing their best to dry their clothes with wads of paper towels. I found an empty stall in the back, and although it was much dirtier than any public restroom I remembered ever being in before, with a few layers of toilet paper along the top of the seat, I found it sanitary enough for my use. I also didn't know how long the rain would have me holed up in the diner, and I had no idea where I'd be able to find a cleaner public restroom in that area of town, at that time of night.

Even though it was a strange place for me to find myself, there was something comforting about sitting there, enclosed within the stall, even as men talked and dried themselves off just a few feet away from where I sat. I wondered if Arthur had ever been to this diner, being as it was one of just a very few restaurants within walking distance to his apartment.

"Walking distance," I repeated, this time out loud, laughing at my selection of words, even if they were just a thought. Someone else thought it was funny, it seemed, as I heard a few men snicker just after they heard me talking to myself on the toilet.

I'd be lying if I said that I wasn't embarrassed at that point, so I made the decision to stay behind the locked door of the stall until those men disappeared. And so I began reading the various examples of graffiti left behind by other men, perhaps some who might have been stuck in an embarrassing situation similar to the one I found myself in.

There were many short poems involving a "man from Nantucket" and a "girl from China." Then there were several different ones containing racial slurs, sexually suggestive phrases and various nicknames. Overall, they contained more swear words than I thought actually existed.

Then one, appearing to be somewhat freshly written, caught my eye. It was neatly located on the back of the door in large, black letters, as if the author really wanted it to be seen by all who used that stall.

Deliverance comes when you take control of that
which has control over you,
When you follow the path around full circle and your
agony is far out of view.
But sometimes when you round the bend, there
comes a DEAD END sign,
And you know if you reached the other side of the
circle, everything would be just fine.

I didn't quite understand it the first time I read
it, nor the second or third. Even though it was a
short piece, I think I was just too tired to make
any sense of anything I read at that point. I
wanted to write it down to analyze later, but I had
nothing to write with and nothing dry to write on.
I read it once more and knew that its simple
words were already memorized.

It made me think of Ms. Carroll, Dylan, and of
Arthur. I imagined it could have been Arthur
himself who wrote those words one night as he
sat here thinking, waiting out the rain that might
drown him outside. I imagined that the message
of the poem, whatever it might actually be saying,
might have pertained to all of them. Maybe, if it
wasn't written by Arthur here, he could possibly
have read it here, maybe even on the night he
died. Or possibly he read it on the wall of some
other dirty restroom, kept it in his head for a
while, and then transcribed it for others to read.

I was just reaching for any relevance. And
either way, was it meant to inspire, or was it the
last breath of a desperate man who was about to

find his own way around all of life's roadblocks?

I could surely see why a man in Arthur's position might be so inclined to write such a note. He was never happy in life. From the day he was born, the only thing that got him through the day was his fruitless pursuit of happiness. And when one too many roadblocks stood in his way, he got off of the road entirely. He realized he would never have the perfect life he always craved. Though he would never admit it, there was one woman he knew deep down inside was his soul mate. She was not glamorous, nor was she simple. She had none of the traditional characteristics that men usually found appealing in a woman, but she was just like him. She was the only woman who could ever get to fully understand a man like Arthur, and only he could really know her.

And now she was dead, and maybe he had felt a little bit guilty about it. And his son, the one thing in life that brought him any pride, was chased away by Arthur's arrogance and temper. The little bit of happiness he found — whether he knew it existed up to that point or not — was now gone. That much he knew.

Ms. Carroll, her life plagued with bad choices made with good intentions, wanted nothing more than a happy family life. But she, like Arthur, was introduced to her soul mate when God created far too many obstacles to ever really join them in happiness. All that came from their temporary and hostile union was a child, who she never got to know.

And from there, that son inherited the misfortune of his parents. Dylan's dreams were just as hopeless. And so were those of his intended bride.

When I was younger, my dad would say, "Shit rolls downhill." That meant that whenever something bad happened in the factory he worked at, the blame would be passed all the way down to the lowest man on the totem pole, and that man would be reprimanded or even fired, simply for doing the job his supervisors demanded of him. Though he liked his job, my dad was always fearful that he would be eliminated because of a mistake made by someone above him. And no matter how hard he tried, he just never seemed to be able to move up in the ranks. Eventually, he couldn't take the politics and the hypocrisy anymore and he quit. He simply walked out on his job, without having another one lined up, and he went out to see what was next for him. Though my mom wasn't happy with his quick decision to become unemployed, my dad found other gainful employment pretty quickly and was happy until he retired from that job several years later.

It seemed like shit was constantly rolling downhill, and Arthur was perched in his chair at the very bottom. He who sits highest of all is He who rolls it all down, and I could now see that I spent my life making excuses for Him. Essentially, I sat just below God on the top of the hill, and I helped roll that shit on down. Arthur eventually found himself unable to advance, and instead of continuing to be covered in shit, he found a way out. Like my dad had done many years ago at the factory, Arthur just quit.

I stepped out from the stall, washed my hands and went back to my table, where my pie and coffee were both cold and waiting for me.

"I thought you might've skipped out already," the waitress said as she approached me from behind. "Let me get you a warm refill on that coffee."

The pie was horrible, and the coffee tasted like it was from yesterday. But I finished them both just as the rain finally ceased. I left the waitress a five-dollar tip, paid my bill at the counter and continued my walk as if I had never even paused at that truck stop.

It was another three miles before I came to where the coroner told me he believed Arthur had died. I thought it would be difficult to locate the exact spot, but the blood that still remained despite of the hard rain was a positive marker.

I tried to imagine what Arthur was thinking just before he pushed himself onto the freeway. What was he feeling as he saw the headlights coming at him? Was it fear of what was next, or fear of the definite pain he would initially feel before he passed on? Or was it a sense of resolution and satisfaction in finally being able to let go of his inner pain and move on to whatever came next for him?

Though not at the level Arthur endured, I understood the pain and uncertainty of a life that seemed to be going nowhere. I had doubts about the one thing in life I had always known to be true. And I doubted my own worth and my own place in this life and the next. Was I just a pawn? Had I ever really helped anybody? Or had I really caused more harm than good in the world?

I pondered these thoughts over and over again all the way home, intermixed with the recitation of that bathroom stall poem I still had not fully understood. I couldn't figure out if I had provided a path around life's obstacles, or if I had actually helped install the roadblocks. Somehow I realized that it was the latter. My beliefs had been a roadblock to my own happiness, and instead of finding a path around it, I justified the obstacle's existence for myself and for others, thus creating more roadblocks.

I was lost. I had no answers to my feelings. And so I quit. I literally quit my stance and my views and my position and my job. I didn't take the time to change out of my dry clothes before I found myself at my writing desk, penning what would be my resignation letter. It was vague and cryptic, I am sure. And the resignation would be effective immediately.

I packed up all my non-priest clothes, stuffed what I could into a military-style duffel bag and emptied that box full of Arthur's money into a zippered duffel bag. I had no idea where I was going as I left the church one last time, but I found myself walking to the bus station.

"Where you heading?" the clerk asked.

"I'm not sure," I responded quite shyly. "Which direction leaves first?"

"There's a bus leaving in fifteen minutes," she said. "It's going west."

"Then west it is."

I still had no idea where I was going, even as I climbed aboard. It was my first trip by bus anywhere, and I knew nothing of my destination. Maybe Arizona; I've always heard Phoenix was nice. Or maybe California. The movies always make it seem just wonderful.

No, scratch that. I needed to see the other side of *my* circle. I'm going to Vegas.